# IT IS ACCEPTABLE

### "DET GÅR AN"

## By Carl Jonas Love Almquist

## 1838

D1733066

## Translated by Michael Timshel

## 2014

Cover art by Gunnar Brusewitz

ISBN-13: 978-1717438447

ISBN-10: 171743844X

Published by Amazon  2018

## A word from the translator

When we read 'It Is Acceptable', or 'Det Går An', as it was called in the original Swedish, we are transported not just across space and time, but across cultures, as well. In this seemingly simple tale of ship-board and road-trip romance, we journey to a time and place where class and social distinctions are so rigid and ingrained, that they are part of the language. Whether you addressed a person in the formal "ni", or the informal "du", depended on your status or class relative to the other person. The wrong choice of 'mamsell' (mademoiselle), or 'fröken' (miss), could result in embarrassment, or even insult. Indeed, these differences are actually a main theme of the story. Today, in America, the "middle-person" is more or less the norm, and we try to be a classless society. But in Sweden of the 1830's, when this was written, the idea of not being in a particular class was revolutionary. And the idea of a man and a woman living together without marrying was just shocking. This is a classic tale that is read by every Swedish high-schooler, but is almost unknown in this country. This translation is dedicated to my daughters, and their daughters, and their daughters, and... MCT

Gunnar Brusewitz

**1838**

## Chapter One

*An engaging and remarkable middle-person. Not a country girl. Not a farm girl at all, but not really of the better class.*

On a beautiful Thursday morning in July, throngs of people streamed past Riddarholm Church, in Stockholm. They were hurrying down the hill between the Court of Appeals and the Government Offices in order to get down to the shores of Lake Mälaren, where the steamboats lay. Everyone was hurrying to the "Yngve Frey", running quickly up the gangway. The hour of departure had already struck. The captain gave the command, "All ashore that's going ashore!"

The visitors bade their departing friends a brief farewell, and went ashore. The gangplank was hauled in, and the steamer headed out. After a few minutes, she was far out in the water.

"This is no good! It's too late! My wife!" muttered one and another traveler to himself sardonically under his breath as they saw the older ladies coming down to the docks. Vigorously waving their kerchiefs and gesturing wildly, they tried to show that they were passengers, and should be aboard. But there were no dinghies to fetch them, and the steamer had already reached Owens. Arrow-quick, it shot past the Military Hospital.

The travelers' mood quickly changed, though, when they heard cries of "Auntie! Auntie!" from a young passenger on the foredeck, who was too shy to shout loudly. Still, they understood that she, unfortunately, had been separated from her aunt, a presumably trusted and pleasant travelling companion.

But people are often so self-centered that they forget the next fellow. People who bought tickets for the salon or afterdeck never ask after the lower classes on the foredeck and fo'c'sle. The "better travelers", this time, were mostly older gentlemen,

5

nearly all with sad faces. They were accompanied by wives and children at that gangly age where the childishness disappears, but has not been replaced with sense and wisdom. Such people are highly egotistical, and for understandable reasons. Well-brought-up children are usually in no condition to help themselves, and must call for help at every instant: a shoe-strap loose, a glove fell into the water, they are hungry again, or thirsty, and the whole world is in disorder for them. Their mothers, therefore, had a lot of difficulty, apart from the exertions they needed to make, just getting themselves up and down the narrow companionways. The family fathers tried to divert themselves with dipping snuff and reading newspapers. But that hardly seemed to suffice. They could not devote much attention to each other, as they were taken up with their own up-keep, their wives, their children. Above all, they must weigh carefully what to eat on board, as not to get really ill. Of all of the natural cures, the soul's pure joy is the best medicine for the body's indisposition and weakness. When that is missing, one is constantly susceptible to everything, and feels ill, both from what one eats, and what one allows to be eaten. Many of the gentlemen still had memories of cholera. It was not too strange that each of them was thinking only about himself. With a seriousness that would have befitted Roman senators, they deliberated, pondered, and discussed. So far as possible they made final plans for food, and other important considerations of their journey.

If there had been any young, unmarried males among the salon-passengers, he probably would have had time to feel sorry for the poor woman on the foredeck, who had been separated from her aunt. He would at least have found out what she looked like, and asked her name.

This time there was no such male among the better folk on the "Yngve Frey". But among the passengers on the foredeck was a handsome young n. c. o. - yes, a sergeant. For economy's sake, or some other reason, he had not asked for anything better than deck-space on this journey. However, because he looked so decent and proper, he was able to mingle with members of the salon-families. They didn't snub him, as his mustachios were dark, upturned, and almost beautiful. His uniform cap was neat enough to not repel the ladies. A certain manliness in his bearing brought the otherwise stiff and aristocratic gentlemen to allow themselves to converse with him, too. He seemed to exude the promise of moving up, in time, to leave the enlisted ranks, and become, if not a captain or a major, then at least a lieutenant.

The kind, young sergeant saw, on the foredeck, the young woman who had been separated from her aunt. He had noticed, when they departed, that she had been wearing a neat little ladies' hat of white cambric. After a while, the hat disappeared and he saw her with a silk shawl over her head like a "Madonna". Question: was this passenger upper or lower class? And whichever she was: why did she change head-covering?

The sergeant became interested in her because of her first mishap. He began to spend all the more time on the foredeck, where he rightly belonged. More and more he abandoned conversation with the salon-nobility...

"I believe," he said to himself, "that pretty girl is of the middle-class. She is probably from the country. She is on her way home, and should have had the company of an older relative, who was hindered from reaching the steamer in time, by her coffee cup. She hid her station in life by taking off the hat. In that way she avoided the unsuitability of travelling without an escort. By putting on the shawl, she made herself into a servant girl. Just like the other four or five girls here on the foredeck, she could travel the length of Lake Mälaren without her aunt, and without scandal."

The sergeant didn't know if he had figured it out correctly or not. Still, he was captivated by the little scene. He couldn't decide if the girl was of higher or lower class than he was, but she was quite smart, and pretty looking in her dark blue coat. The big scarf of fine, pink, almost white silk, with narrow, green stripes here and there was knotted under her chin, and tastefully

7

arranged at the neck. That appealed to the sergeant, and he didn't long for the white cambric hat. He went down to the captain to find out her name. After looking at the passenger list for a while, it showed that her name was Sara Videbeck, and that she was the daughter of a master glazier from Lidköping. That was unusually detailed information on a passenger list. As it turned out, she had a passport, which steamer passengers seldom had, and for safety's sake, she had entrusted it to the captain for the trip.

The sergeant sat deep in thought in the dining room. Look at the dining room! It is there that the foredeck-passengers must crowd into at meal times, if they are sufficiently brave and bold. It was now about breakfast-time. Or it could be, if one ordered something. The sergeant reasoned like this: A master glazier's daughter from Lidköping. It's a small town, far, far from Stockholm. A bourgeois girl? In a way, yes. A daughter of the bourgeoisie, but of the lowest bourgeois class. A captivating, and remarkable middle-thing. An engaging and remarkable middle-person. Not a country girl. Not a farm girl at all, but not really of the better class. How does one think of such persons? What are they called? There was something unknowable about this middle-sort.

"Let's see... bring me a steak!" Breakfast provided a much-needed pause in the sergeant's wandering, disorganized train of thought. When he finished his steak he continued to himself: "Of course, dammit, she's just like me. For example, what am I? Not a soldier. Not an officer. Not lesser, nor really better. Let me see...damn...bring me a porter!"

After the porter, the sergeant stood up, stroked his mustachios into crooks, spat deeply into the left salon corner, and paid for breakfast.

"Hmm...," he thought, Sara Vid... Vid... has had nothing to eat this morning. I'd like to go up on deck, and see if I can talk to her. For instance, invite her to breakfast.

The sergeant's train of thought, (now, as before, a little wandering), dissolved into a pause. He inspected his boots, and found them shiny, his uniform cap brushed nice and clean. With two lithe bounds up the companionway, the slim young warrior was on deck again. He looked around, and set course for the bow.

The first his gaze fell upon was a group of Dalacarlia-girls. They stood in front of the previously-mentioned four or five serving girls, including one with a pink scarf, and beyond, were a couple of grimy machines. The sergeant approached. He heard the Dala-girls offering horse-hair rings for sale; black, white, green, with a name or a motto artfully woven in. They wanted the other girls to buy, but the serving girls were tough and wanted to haggle. He didn't hear the one with the pink scarf haggle, but he did see her carefully picking through the horse-hair rings. At last, she settled on a smooth black and white one, with no lettering at all. The Dala-girl set her price; six shillings. The Pink Scarf nodded in agreement. She brought out a little purse, a bag knitted from green silk, from her coat pocket. A silver coin appeared in her hand. It lay nicely on the lilac glove. The coin was Sweden's smallest denomination in silver, twelve shillings. "Can you give me six shillings in change?" asked a lovely voice with a West-Goth accent of the most beautiful kind, with just a little rolling of her r's.

"Six shillings change? Oh, sweetie, I don't have it! You want to buy two rings, and that would be twelve shillings. Buy two! Buy two!"

He heard "No, but…" from the Pink Scarf.

The sergeant stood back and could only see the backs of their necks. He assumed that the answer came from the one with her head raised a little forward. The sergeant sauntered up and said, "Permit me, Mademoiselle Vid… (He caught himself) permit me to…hm… buy the two horse-hair rings from the poor Dala-girl. He laid a twelve-shilling in the Dala-girl's hand, and without further ceremony, took both black-and-white rings that the girl was holding up in hopes of a sale. The Pink Scarf looked up in surprise at the soldier. But he immediately and unabashedly took the one ring that she had previously chosen, gave it to her, and said, "Is this the one you like? Please take it and keep it. I will keep the other."

The girl looked at him with what he thought were really beautiful eyes. She accepted the ring he handed her with amazement. But when he thought she would put the ring on, which she had intended at first, she instead drew over to the railing. Without saying a word she dropped it into the lake.

"Well done, Sergeant!" he said to himself. "That tells me that you've been properly shot down. Bravo sir! Why should I call her 'mademoiselle' when she disguises herself with a scarf? She should be spoken to familiarly and addressed as 'du', if it's like that. And why offer an unknown girl a ring. And to do it on deck! Damn, Albert!"

He went to the opposite railing, and threw in the other horse-hair ring, which he had already set on his finger, into the water. He spat on the salute-cannon sitting nearby. Then he strolled back toward the stern. When he came around to the foredeck again, it happened that he came just opposite the unknown Pink Scarf, who was standing watching the machinery's movements.

"See," he said and held out his hands. "I threw my ring into the lake too. It was the best we could do."

First a sharply measuring look from head to toe, but then a barely perceptible but really nice smile. A fine, effervescent expression, that immediately disappeared, was her answer.

"Is the ring in the lake? Oh then," she added.

"I hope a pike has already eaten it," said the sergeant.

"A big perch got mine."

"When the pike eats the perch, which I hope is soon, then both rings will lie under the same heart."

Those last words were whispered with a tenderness that completely failed for the sergeant. The girl turned on her heel, and blended into the crowd of other girls.

"Fantastic, Boss!" he said to himself. Shot down again! And why speak from the heart? And on deck? But I'm glad, at least, that she wasn't offended when I dared to address her as 'du'. And for that then: never 'mademoiselle' again!"

He went down to the dining room, and bought a cigar, which he lit and returned to the deck. He sat on his trunk, with his face turned up, relaxed and free, drawing long clouds of smoke from his cigar. He looked superb.

He noticed that the lovely glassmaster's daughter walked indifferently by. Sometimes she adjusted the pink silk scarf, and fingered the corners that fell down over her chest. She was talking animatedly with the other girls, and looked completely unselfconscious.

The cigar came to its end, as do many things in this world. The sergeant threw the little butt, aiming for the lake, but it was so light that it only flew a little way onto the deck and it lay there smoking. Presto! Out came a foot with the very neatest, shiniest boot and stamped it out. The sergeant raised his eyes from the foot up to the person, and saw that it was the 'Unknown'. Her eyes met his. The sergeant hurried up from his trunk, went up to her, and with a polite bow said "Thank you sweet miss! My cigar was not worthy of the young lady's foot, but…"

A cold, dismissive expression was her only answer. She turned her back and left.

"So, to hell with her!" With that thought, the sergeant reddened, and leapt down the companionway to the dining room. He crept into the darkest corner, suitable for sleep, or observation. "Dammit, Albert!" He thought, stroking the hair away from his face. "I called her 'miss'. She liked that as little as when I called her 'mademoiselle'. Mischief!"

He was not alone in the room; therefore he did not speak aloud, or even half-aloud. But, to hastily prove his courage, both to the others, and to himself, he barked harshly at the girl at the counter, "Sandwich with salted meat on it! Right now!" The waitress came with the order on a tray. "Go to hell with this sandwich! Didn't I order one on a French roll?

Obediently and meekly, she went back with her tray, and moved the crisp-bread sandwich to the sideboard.

"A glass of Haut-Brion, Miss! And don't make me wait! The glass was filled, and placed alongside a new sandwich on a French roll.

"Does she think I am supposed to try to fit the whole roll in my mouth? In Stockholm they have the sense to cut a roll in two, and butter each side. The waitress came back, took a knife, and began to cut the bread.

"No…I ask you the Devil's pretty-please, get a new French roll, cut it, and butter it on the inside. There's already butter on the outside! Get a new roll. What a long time to wait! Dammit… throw the whole thing away. I'm not hungry.

The waitress at the sideboard mumbled something about snooty passengers. The sergeant didn't blame her. He went over, and paid for the sandwiches. "I ordered them. See, here is the money."

"You have stomach problems… yes, yes," said a black-clad passenger. The sergeant turned around, and recognized the pale, but shining face, with two round, pale blue, bird-like eyes, as the pastor in Ulricehamn. "Aha. I am your humble servant. It's pastor Su… headed back east, no doubt."

"Yes, yes, I am."

"I am travelling to West-Gothland, too, but that's not going home for me, but away," said the sergeant. Mechanically, he picked up the big, disputed but paid-for sandwich, and opened wide to take a bite.

"So it goes," said the pastor. "The one travelling up, and the other, down. I'm on my way to Ulricehamn."

"Yes, and…" (the sergeant emptied his glass, still waiting for him on the tray.)

"So long as you have your health, it's good for you to travel to and fro, like that," remarked the pastor.

"Oh, that's true, yes…" (The sergeant swallowed the last of his sandwich).

"Are you leaving Stockholm for a long time?"

"I have three months leave. May I offer to buy you a drink, Pastor? What will you have, porter, or port wine?"

"Yes, yes, but traveling on the lake has troubled my stomach. Maybe Port wine, in any case. Or porter!"

The sergeant ordered both. And the pastor, who was in no shape to decide, drank both. He finished with the warmest and most hospitable invitation for the young soldier to visit at Ulricehamn and Timmelhed to take communion again.

The sergeant bowed and paid for his order. Then he ran back up on deck in a more cheerful mood. When he looked around at the coastlines that the steamer was sailing past, he saw that they were close to Strängnäs. The big cathedral could be seen by the passengers from a long distance away. Its majestic tower dominates the Södermanland landscape far and wide. Only when you get closer, do you see the group of small, red wooden houses, asymmetrically bunched under the church. Only the red checkered high-school and schoolhouse, by their height, constituted a break in the other ramshackle hovels. When you finally put in at the beat-up old docks and stops, you say to yourself: "This is Strängnäs."

FOOTNOTE: [1]
The unusual scene that happened here; that a serving-girl prepares a crisp-bread sandwich, and when she is justly reminded to make it with light bread, makes it without cutting it, constitutes telling evidence of the meekness of the restaurateur to allow an ignorant country-girl even once to attempt. Learning's first steps are often difficult, and one gets upbraided. May each and every one step up and take the path of noble patience, as seen here!

## Chapter 2

*There was nothing aristocratic here, neither of the high-born*
*House of Lords sort, nor of the wealthy commoners of a rich and*
*proud bourgeoisie, nor of the old prominent families among the*
*independent farmers…*

The passengers, looking up from the docks did not have a harbor
or a landing before them, nor a real street, but a riverbank. Most
of the houses were discourteous enough to turn their gable-ends
toward the street. Because the steamer was to stop, perhaps for a
half hour, they went ashore. One isn't greeted with pretzels here,
like they do in Södertälje. But, if you step carefully when you
put your foot on the dock, watch out, and don't step in a hole
between the rotten planks, you can make it up to town with your
life intact.

That was the case with the sergeant, and with one other. You
see, when he stood on the foredeck and saw the gangplank run
out, he noticed the Pink Scarf a little ways off. The Pink Scarf
was looking up at the little town with twinkling eyes. He grew
bold again. He decided to avoid all the dangerous words;
"Miss", and "Mademoiselle", and any other title.

"A word," he turned, and said breezily, "Come, let's go ashore!
It's too chaotic here on board. They're going to load wood, and
it'll be busy here. It's awful in the dining salon, too. It's
unpleasant to eat down there… hmm…I know a really nice,
decent place here in Strängnäs. I think I could go for some
breakfast after such a long fast."

She let him take her by the arm, walked down the gangplank,
and as they crossed the rickety dock, she held close to him. And
– now they stood in Strängnäs.

"I really like this little town," she said breezily, looking happily
around. This is completely different from Stockholm!"

"As we get further into town, it's really nice," answered the
sergeant.

"Look, look!" she continued, "Oh, it's breath-taking... but... yes...oh yes...Lidköping is yet prettier."

The young soldier was delighted to quickly, and unexpectedly hear that his acquaintance was a chatty person. He started to think that Strängnäs was fairly nice, too. In fact, it was. All without pretension. You come up from the lake, and walk only narrow, crooked alleys, or streets, winding over the hills. Straight streets weren't seen in this community. The little houses are old and common. You find soon that not just the gables, but the long sides have covered windows too, and doors where one might want to go in. There was nothing aristocratic about these houses; neither of the high-born House-of-Lords sort, nor of the wealthy commoners of a rich, and proud bourgeoisie, nor of the old prominent families among the independent farmers. No, one sees only the civil, unpretentious sort. You would believe that all of the houses belong to glass-masters, boat captains, brush-makers, and fishermen.

It was clear that this pertained only to the Strängnäs, that passengers met coming from the lake. It surrounded him before he got as far as the cathedrals forested hill, in whose neighborhood the bishop's house and others indicate a higher world. But the sergeant, with his glass-master girl, had not yet reached those heights. They had not even reached the square. Because of her exclamation about the little houses with the white window frames, they had stayed in the remarkable Strängnäs labyrinth of little, crooked streets and houses that lie between the shore and the square. He directed his companion to the high stairway that led from the street itself, down to a yard. They crossed the yard to the door of the house.

"Here," whispered the sergeant, "lives a rich painter, who runs a really nice hospitality-house. Let's go inside, and see how nice it is.

The girl seemed quite at home, but she often added that Lidköping was yet prettier. They crossed the porch, came into the house, and up a new stairway. It led into a big room with a sideboard on the second floor. It was, therefore, a sort of an inn,

thought Sara Videbeck. The sergeant went over to pretty, cheerful looking person wiping dishes by the counter. "Let us have a small room here... and breakfast. What do you have?
"Raspberries and cream."
"Anything more substantial?"
"Fried woodcock... fresh salmon..."
"Yes, that's fine, but hurry up." "And (whispered the sergeant, as he led his companion into the left alcove, while continuing to speak to the person with the dishes through the door,) a couple of glasses of cherry wine!"
When they settled into the alcove, and for sake of comfort closed the door in case others should come into the main room, Sara Videbeck took off her silk shawl. She showed a head of shining, dark brown hair, parted straight, and without a single loose lock at the temples. The sergeant remembered that they had disappeared together with the cambric hat. But a couple of separate, nicely arranged locks fell behind her ears. She pulled off her lilac gloves, and revealed two white, plump hands. They didn't look like they were accustomed to hard work, but one could see that they were a little broad. The lovely fingers, with little dimples at the joints were a little plump, too. The sergeant decided that these fingers had never touched a lute or a keyboard, held an artist's brush, or turned the pages of fine books (for which slim, supple fingertips are preferred). He was even surer that they had never pushed a shovel, cleaned stable, washed clothes, or such. He left unsaid if they, in their days, had kneaded window putty, for window putty leaves the skin white and soft. So much for the hands. The rest of the person was not at all short, or rotund, but was fairly thin and tallish.
The girl was not uncomfortable, alone with the sergeant. She broke off a little lavender sprig from a pot in the window, rubbed it between her hands, and sniffed her fingers with delight. The sergeant, not to be idle, broke off a geranium leaf and did the same with it.

"What a nice, lovely room!" she exclaimed, "and look what a fine chest of drawers. Is it walnut, or oak? No, it is certainly polished pear wood... could it be apple?

The sergeant, who had never been at home in a woodworking shop, could not say one way or another. Instead, he turned his attention to another object and burst out: "Indeed! A broad, gilded frame around the mirror! But it is as it is. It ought to be mahogany."

"Mahogany? Oh! I know what would be better: to make the frame around the mirror of glass too. Make it of thin, clear crown-glass, strips left over from cutting the panes. You put them together on the whole frame and put colored paper underneath. Picture it: You can see yourself in the mirror, but in the frame you can see yourself just for fun. Also, you can use whatever paper you wish. It could be really pretty. Have... have... haven't seen it?

She seemed not really be able to come upon how she should address him; formally or not. Just then the waitress came in: a soft, white but coarsely-woven cloth was laid on the table, and upon it freshly dried plates.

"But what if the steamer leaves without us?"

"Oh, no." answered the sergeant, "Before that, they fire a signal-shot, and before the sound dies away, we always make it to the landing."

The girl who had brought the dishes had left and shut the door. The sergeant lifted his glass of cherry wine and said "Skål to the journey!"

Sara Videbeck took the other little glass, clinked it with her host's and said, "Thanks!"

"A word before we drink," interjected the sergeant. "It's difficult and tiresome to not know how to address each other... and so... I'd never want to make anyone sad or angry or shocked... and... for example, couldn't we address each other... for example familiarly with 'du'... so long as we are eating, at least, or..."

"Du… yes, that would be okay." With these words she clinked glasses one more time. The matter was decided, and cherry wine was drunk.

The sergeant was like a new man after that stone fell from his chest. He walked around the room, twice as relaxed, and happy. But the beautiful glassmaster's daughter, on the other hand, underwent not the slightest change. She sat at the table and ate, and served herself, certainly in a really pleasant way, but not with any higher grace. He addressed his new acquaintance with "du" in every eighth word, with neither shyness nor formality. She looked endlessly at ease. The sergeant, who at least by his behavior, felt excellent, and just got happier, and said, "Dear Sara, a little more raspberries?" Isn't this cream really good?"

"First rate! Thanks! I remember down at Lundsbrunn last summer…"

He went out and ordered some more raspberries.

At that instant the signal-shot rang out from the steamer.

"See there?" she said, got up and put on her gloves. "Cancel the raspberries."

"Dear Sara, sit! The raspberries will be right here. We'll probably make it down to the boat."

"No no! It is best to be punctual. Ask how much it cost," she added, put on her shawl, and pulled out a handkerchief which contained her purse.

"What?" he interjected, "It is I who… quick, quick!" She brushed past him to the counter in the main hall, and asked how much the meal had cost.

"One riksdalar and twenty-four shillings."

"Here, dear mademoiselle, (she took from her green silk purse), are thirty-six shillings, by my calculations, that makes half. Goodbye, miss!" she nodded afterwards to the waitress. The nod, both to the 'mademoiselle', and the 'miss', was friendly, but a little superior, and implied that she didn't much care for either of them.

The sergeant, for his part, wanted to stammer out that it was he who invited, and absolutely must pay. However, Sara was already out the door. Time was passing. He laid out his thirty-six shillings, bit his lip in irritation and followed her out.

After they came to the porch, walked through the yard, and were about to climb the stairs back up to the street, she made a little movement that indicated that the sergeant should take her arm, and he did.

"Thanks for bringing me to this lovely place," she said half-aloud in the sweetest voice. She touched his hand with hers like a gentle clap. Did you say a rich painter lives here? Well!"

"Nothing to thank for," he answered. "You paid for your own!" he added to himself, feeling mortified.

"Yes, you shall have my great thanks. I was really hungry. Where there are neat, polite people is where you want to go. And this town is called Strängnäs?"

"Yes. I would like to take you up to the cathedral to look at the greater part of the city; where they have beautiful, shady trees to stroll under."

"Oh, go on! No, we must get down to the steamer. It's already waiting."

As they walked with cheerful steps through the criss-crossing alleys, Sara waved happily at every little corner they passed. Right as it was, she asked, "How did you know that my name is Sara? Also, I'd like to know your first name."

"Albert," answered the sergeant.

"Albert... Let me see...Yes, that's right. I've seen it in the almanac. That was how my godson, Master-carpenter Ahlgren's boy, was christened last summer. He's a special boy, as you shall see, Albie. Eyes bright as enamel."

"Are you from Lidköping? And presumably going there now?" the sergeant permitted himself to ask.

"Careful! Watch your step!" she said, for they were now on the fragile quay. But, they made their way to the gangplank without incident, and found themselves in the world of the steamship, anew. The moorings were cast, and the paddlewheels began to turn around. With a cloud of smoke, and muffled thunder, the swimming dragon bade adieu to Strängnäs.

## Chapter 3

*"He who would cut glass, sir, must have a diamond!"*

The sergeant was determined to show his acquaintance a courtesy. He went, therefore, down to the dining hall, and asked for a pound of candy. "Those aren't available on a steamer," answered the man. "Well, goddam! Are there any oranges? Like the ones lying right there in that basket?"
"Yes."
"Good, give me four of them."
When he went, with his fruit in his hand, he found the deck fully crowded, and arranged in the following way: The greater part of the 'better' people – gentlemen, ladies and children, - had gone down to the salon. A few couples sat on the afterdeck, not exactly in lively conversation, but they weren't asleep, either. On the other hand, they didn't care much about what was going on around them. The Dala girls, farthest forward in the bow, had made beds on the coiled-up hawsers, sleeping. The four or five previously mentioned girls had collected with their backs against a partially folded sail. The captain was probably in his cabin. He wasn't to be seen on deck. The mechanic was in his engine-room. "Where, then, is my 'pink'?"
"He discovered her, at last, sitting on a green-painted deck chair that stood by the railing in the lee of one of the wheel cowlings. The sergeant had nothing against such a secluded place. He walked over with his oranges, sat next to her, and offered her one. She nodded thanks, and picked up her purse. "God-damn-son-of-a-bitch!" thought the sergeant, as the blood rushed to his face. "Does she want to pay for the oranges now, bang, just like that? This petit-bourgeoisie, I don't give a ..."
But it wasn't as bad as that. She took a knife with a silver handle out of her crocheted purse, and peeled an orange with it, which she politely handed to Albert. Then she peeled one for herself, cut it into six pieces, and began to enjoy the flavor.

"Thanks, dear Sara!" said Albert, accepting his orange. Then he asked to borrow her knife to cut up his fruit. He looked at the knife with a bit of wonder. It was oddly blunt, quite round on the end, without looking like a table-knife. Also, it was new and very sharp on one edge. He gave it no further attention, but said, after a while, "Now, Sara, we must get better acquainted and you should tell me how closely related you are to your aunt, the one who..."

"Didn't come with me this morning? I don't think it's hard to say how closely related I am to my aunt."

"Yes. Certainly, but..."

"Yes, I am really sorry that she didn't catch the boat, poor Aunt Ulla. She'll have to get a ride on her own, now, or take the Gothenburg train. Let's see where we can meet it along the way, if we can at all. Maybe she'll stay in Stockholm, now that the trip began so badly for her. I have another aunt, too, you might as well know. She is a maiden-lady named Gustava. She lives in Lidköping, and cares for my sick mother while I am away. But, my aunt Ulla has been a Stockholmer for a long time. She just wanted to go home with me to shake loose a little. It's too bad she made herself late, but she often does that, poor Aunt Ulla. I was sorry for my own sake, too. It's always good to have an aunt, or someone, along when you're out travelling. But I was sure that it wouldn't go wrong, if I met some traveler on the way who... eat, Albie! I'm not going to eat all this by myself!"

"Thanks," he said, glad to get a word in, too. "Do you travel to Stockholm often? It is indeed a long way between Stockholm and Lidköping."

"I had never been to Stockholm before. I needed to, this time, to look at oil and diamonds, and to see the latest styles."

The sergeant looked wonderingly at the girl, and said nothing. "Oil?" he thought. I must be completely and totally mistaken about her. "Hmm. The latest styles?" He measured her figure from top to toe. It was certainly really elegant, in its way. At last he said, half aloud, "Diamonds?"

"Yes, indeed, diamonds, sir! Ha, ha...you think, maybe, that flint would do. No, no, no. Flint is okay enough for striking sparks, such as in the flintlock of a gun. But, you see, he who would cut glass, sir, must have a diamond!" With these words her eyes opened, and shone as if with an inborn self-esteem. She looked almost proud, although pride never otherwise showed itself in her expression, except on the occasion when she turned her back on someone. She sank immediately back into familiarity again when she saw that Albert was on his way to dropping his orange in astonishment. She added, "We have always gotten the chalk from Gothenburg, otherwise, and could have gotten the oil there, too. But my mom got a letter saying that it could be gotten in Stockholm for twelve shillings cheaper per keg. So, it amused me to come up here and check on it, because I had an aunt here to stay with. But the new style that they talk about so much in Lidköping. How up in Stockholm, they have started making colored glass for church windows. I don't care. I haven't seen any in Stockholm. I purposely visited every church in the city, and it wasn't an easy task, because they are insufferably numerous. There wasn't colored glass in a single one. I don't know where that lie came from, if not from Uppsala, where an assessor is said to be painting the window in an apse. On the other hand, I'd like to learn to do that, as we have orders for church windows even...yes... all the way down to Skara. There is no one who could handle glass in Skara, and I knew it would be a good deal if we could color glass in the shop. We would then be the only ones in the area who could work in the new style. And they would come to us, as soon as anything cracked in the church. Never mind that. I have heard that that style isn't used anywhere, and when it is, it's worthless. I did find diamonds, and I'm fairly pleased with the trip. And oil, then..."

"But what in God's name do you use so much oil for?"

"For glazing putty, is all I know. What else would it be for?"

"Why doesn't your father travel himself on such important, long-distance business?"

"Oh God! He's been dead for six years, now."

"That's different."

"And my mother, poor thing, has run the shop, since then, in her right as a widow, of course. But she has lain in bed for two years, so I can say that I run it alone."

"But tell me, pretty Sara, how old are you, if I dare ask?"

"Twenty-four years, and a little more."

"What? Is it possible? I took you for eighteen. Such cheeks... such skin…"

"Yes. The same cheeks I had when I was eighteen. They say that accountant's daughters, and working women of higher and lower class, seem younger than they are. That's what I heard at Lund's Spa. But I don't think there's anything all that great about looking older at a young age. It's much better the other way around. How old are… if I dare ask?"

"Me? We are about the same age. I am twenty-five."

"And I took you for just nineteen and not even graduated yet, you seem so open and self-assured."

"Yes, my dear, to be honest, I haven't graduated, and probably never will."

" What…what are you?"

"Just a non-com."

"I've seen non-coms before among the regimental types, and they were honest fellows. I remember at Lund's Spa…where I saw lay-abouts go up to the young ladies, pretending to drink toasts with mineral water. There were also a swarm of West Goth- and regimental lieutenants, captains, majors and such that they call officers. They, too, pretended to be in ill health, and chatted-up the young ladies. But if I ever saw any non-commissioned officers, they were always real men who really were sick, and drank the water for comfort's sake."

"What were you doing at Lund's Spa, Sara? You are so healthy. You must have gone there to enjoy the beautiful country-side."

"I was just there for one day, to sell boxes. I had to go there to check on a couple of our apprentices, they had sent for to install a whole lot of window panes. They had gotten knocked out in a wildly thrown ball on the fourth of July. One is never safe about boys. They beat up the merchandise. They can't cut glass, either. They handle the diamond poorly. Because it was a large job, I went out there myself, and I'm not sorry. What do you think, Albert? I set fifty-six small panes, twenty-two of cheaper green glass. And listen!...thirty four of fine table glass. Also I sold ten glass boxes, made only by us at the work-shop, with gold paper under the trim. And I sold six big lanterns, to light the way for them when they go down in the cellar for seltzer water and mineral water and kreutzervrimmel, and such. Like I said, I only saw two non-coms there, serious guys with gout, West Goths, both of them. How did you become a non-commissioned officer so young?"

"They have young non-coms in Stockholm sometimes... particularly those... yeah, you see, I am actually not far from an officer... I'm a sergeant."

"Schersant? Well, that's just as well. Never aspire to be an officer, or lieutenant and such. What do those lazy-bones do, but talk bullshit to the ladies in the day-time and with the serving girls at night. Crap! Collars and gold braid, bills unpaid."

Pause.

The soldier sat a little stunned at hearing his open-hearted friend's eloquent, audacious diatribe. He, himself, did not know if he wanted to be a lieutenant all that much. He had hoped to get promoted with the help of secret association with a certain large family in the capital. He knew also that, for the present, his finances were in good shape for the, sort-of, inspection tour of certain properties, where he had been dispatched during his vacation. Therefore, he didn't want to let himself be bothered by the dreary rhyme: "Collars and gold braid, etc." But he could not deny that sometimes he liked all that rigmarole with titles that indicate social standing, such as 'mademoiselle' and 'miss'. He blinked, aghast, therefore, at Sara's opinionated outburst. He looked her in the face; the happy, friendly eyes seemed to stand in contradiction to the strongly worded speech. When he regarded the plump, red, beautifully shaped lips, with the even, glimmering white teeth, and occasionally-glimpsed little red tongue-tip, a man like him could be forgiven the silent question: "Has no one in the world ever kissed those lips?"

Sara looked him in the face, as he had looked at hers, and finally asked in a mild voice, "What are you looking at?"

Quite spontaneously, and boldly he answered, "I was sitting here wondering if anyone had ever kissed those lips."

A fleeting smile was her only answer, and she looked out over Lake Mälaren. There was no trace of coquetry, or any glimpse of ill-will, but on the other hand, nothing romantic, or heavenly. It was a middle thing of an unexplainable sort. It was neither ugly, nor deeply beautiful. It was like the kind of which one usually says with a happy face, "Oh, it's okay!"

Encouraged that, at least, she did not reject him, and turn her back and walk away, the sergeant continued, "I could say a lot, dear Sara, of the same sort of things that you, yourself spoke of; that one says 'mamsell' and 'miss', and I even admit that I am not unaccustomed to that way of speaking. But you have declared to me how you hate it. I don't want to mention the heart even once, as I remember from before... and besides, I think, to be honest, your heart is made of glass, and I, I don't have a diamond in my arsenal, the only weapon that can make a mark on it."

"Are you going to stay in Arboga? The steamer leaves for there tomorrow, Albert," she asked with a penetrating look.

"Me? No, certainly not. I am going to Vadsbo parish to inspect some property, and then perhaps further into West Gothland. "

"Then we'll travel together, (again, a penetrating look)... we can get a couple of horses for a two seat buggy... and we'll split the cost... and... for I see that you have no transportation with you. Farm wagons are awful to ride on, beside some scoundrel of a wagon driver. They aren't my people. They are seldom clean.

The sergeant jumped up, and would well have clasped her in his arms, if they had not been on deck. "She has a heart!" he thought.

"Sit down, Albert, and we'll amuse ourselves with figuring out the travel expense. Help me, if I get it wrong; my biggest pleasure is mental arithmetic. Let's see now: The first leg, starting from Arboga is to Fellingsbro?"

The sergeant sat down by her side, cheerful and elated as if he had gotten carte blanche. And she was, at that moment, as radiant, or, more rightly, as sweetly, beautiful as a girl... to his taste... could ever be. She was so sensible and wise, and yet so engaging.

"Well, aren't you going to answer me?" she asked, and smacked him lightly with her lilac colored glove, which she had been careful to take off before peeling the orange.

"The road runs right to Fellingsbro, and from there to Glanshammar," he said.

"So, Vretstorp?"

"No, no, no. We have to go through Örebro and Kumla, first."

"And Vretstorp, that is for sure. Then Bodarne and Hova, and then we are home."

"What, you live in Hova?"

"I am at home in West Gothland, and as soon as I set foot on the ground in Hova, I'm as good as home." Herewith, Sara stretched out one little foot, and put it decisively, and West Gothicly, down on the deck.

Albert got a fresh opportunity to admire the well made, beautiful high-buttoned shoe. "Is that Lidköping work?" he asked.

"What do you mean?"

"I mean, if they have such good shoe-makers in Lidköping, that..."

"It is a handsome; yes, a rare city! Have you never been to Lidköping? ...shoe-makers?...oh, then! We have tailors, metal artisans and blacksmiths, decorative case makers, carpenters, we have everything. We even have shopping, and a rich restaurateur, on the street a ways to the left of the plaza.

However, I hold a bad opinion of such people who live on other people's downfall, and wastefulness. Hand work, on the other hand, makes that which works and lasts in the world. Where do the restaurateur's wares go? He is a commissioner of the Gothenburg Railroad, and has a great big, ballroom, where officers with mamsells and young ladies hold court. Ballroom dances are really something, as you shall see! But I still don't like tavern operations; if people were folks, then people like that would have to move out of Lidköping, and away. But the way it is now, a lot of people like to drink, and play music, and dance, and... it's an absurdly large dance hall, Albert! It has eight casement windows in a row, as I recall; and twenty-four panes in each window!"

"Don't you like to dance at all, Sara?"

"When I have closed up shop, and I'm done for the day, and I'm all by myself, then sometimes I dance, but then it's without a violin."

"Now that's a real, proper, West-Goth girl!" thought the sergeant. But she seemed so endlessly mild, so touching at that moment, that he said nothing. After a few moments he added, "About your mother; she's so ill, Sara, what if we find when we... when you arrive, that she has died?"

"Yes, if God wills, poor thing! She has no real joy in life. She's had constant trouble, and sorrow, and now, at the end, mostly sickness. It's not good, Albert."

"That's a story that is way too sad. But if she lies on her death-bed, what will happen with your work-shop?"

"Yes, then my right to it will end, and I will get nothing from the magistrate, I know that, but I have thought about it, anyway."

"So?"

"Oh, I might as well tell you," she continued, as she edged a little closer to Albert on the bench, and looked around, as if she feared some unauthorized listener should hear her secrets. When the deck, as previously mentioned, was clear of people, she turned again to him, looking confidential and wise, and waving

28

her little glove in the air, sometimes gently slapping his arm with it.

"I have figured out how a girl without parents or siblings, such as me, can live, and live well..." she said. I have linens and clothing to last for many years, and they won't wear out much, which they don't, if one is careful. When my mother passes, I may no longer cut glass into panes, and putty them in large buildings, and new construction, those go to the master craftsmen. But there's an art, you know, that no one in Lidköping can do better than I do, for I have developed, on my own, a blend of chalk and oil in the right dimensio... no, proportions... (one says dimensions about the length and breadth of the glass itself. One says proportions of the correct mixing, and amounts of chalk and oil together. The words are only used in our trade, and you don't understand them, Albert)... well, I just want to say that I have worked out the proportions for that mixture, that no one knows but me, that makes a putty so strong, that not even the bitterest of Fall rains can dissolve it. I shall make it, and sell it to all the glass-masters, who shall buy it in Lidköping, Vännerborg, and Mariestad, if they can only learn about it. And they know about it already, for I have had my boys trumpet it on their out-of-town work. At home, I shall sell it out of my office.

"But as an unmarried woman, you are defenseless, and...!

"We'll see about that. With a mean drunk, like my mother had, poor thing, then I would be defenseless and miserable. No, actually, I'll take care of myself, just as I am. The little place in Lidköping, I'll tend to myself. It's a fairly small, wood-framed house, like one of those in Strängby... snug...how was it... yes..."

"Strängnäs."

"And when Mama passes on, the place will be mine. Poor Mother! She'll probably live on for a couple more years. At any rate, the mayor tells me, I and the house and land won't need defending, even if I am not married. The house doesn't provide

29

much income, although I could rent out a couple of rooms upstairs, and live on the bottom floor, myself."

"Since I like to have a little fun and be around people, and I don't want to just sit around all the time, I'll open a little shop, with sales, where women can work, one that has not been brought into a formal guild. I intend to sell, in my store, fine, beautiful little boxes of glass, with underlayments of colored paper. I have made them for several years, and they're all the rage with the country folk, for miles around. Also, I make lamps and lanterns. Indeed, I have learned to adhere foil to glass, so I can make little mirrors for everyone in the parish. Perhaps I'll take in all kinds of retail goods, to sell on commission, like woven goods, and linen fabrics, handkerchiefs, scarves, and home-spun. I'll just have to be careful about silk, as it under guild control. It'll be pretty good business, if one is nice to the customers at the counter, and I'll sit in my shop from ten in the morning, until five in the afternoon. It's not worth it to stay longer. Before ten in the morning, I get all my boxes and glass items ready. In the evening I mix putty for all the glass-masters. It'll be good business and a good life!"

Sara's eyes and lips and cheeks were aglow. "Shall you sit inside the whole year, and never get out to look around, and breathe the wonderful fresh country air?"

"At sunrise I go out on the road to Truve. I do that every morning of the summer, preferably when the weather is clear."

"Tru... what is that?"

"I know that it is Truve. It is Richeft's beautiful estate on Mariestad Road. If only the road between there and town weren't so terribly sandy. But, I don't care so much. I don't go that way very often. Many mornings I just like to just sit at home. I have salvia and roses in the windows, and I'm going to get some potted lavenders. Also, I can see the Lida River out the window, and there's nothing more beautiful. If I want to see more water, I have great Lake Vännern to view when I look out my window towards the gap at Kållands Island, and I have that, if I just look toward the town bridge."

"And when you grow old, pretty Sara?"

"If I live to be fifty, I think I'll start travelling to the market with my wares. For, so long as I'm young, it's better to stay home in my little shop."

"One likes to go up to a store counter where such a pretty business-lady is sitting," he admitted.

"But the times when it's nasty out to try to travel to the market," she continued, a little turned away, "one runs into... yes. If I get to fifty, I think it'll be about hanging on. On the other hand, business will be lighter at home in the shop, then I'll want to try at the market, if I haven't put together a sum of money by then, I can live without want. That's what I hope for. For, one can live very nicely and feel really good as long as ..." (here her face fell and her expression darkened).

"Well, my God! What are you talking about?"

"Oh, yes. I mean, as long as you watch out not to get a parasite, who eats up and squanders at whim and in laziness, what one has amassed by toil and determination. What's the point in being orderly when the blighter is all the more disorganized, and gluts himself on the labor of the industrious? And how can one work with joy and enthusiasm, when one has no joy in their heart; when anxiety sits in their throats..."

"I don't understand you."

"So? Hmm."

"For God's sakes, say what you mean!"

"Yes, I can tell you the whole story, I guess. I was out one Michaelmas eve with my mom. It was fall, and the wind was blowing her hair around her hood. In despair, she ran up to the big city bridge that spans the Lida River in our city. I was fifteen years old. I ran after her. I was afraid that in her dreadful agony, she would jump into the water. However, when I reached her, she stopped, and took me in her arms, stood at the bridge gate, and looked around. There were no pedestrians about. 'For your sake I'll refrain," she whispered. "I shall live on in pain until you are a little bigger. But, woe and damnation over this one. At least I'll be quit of him!' With that, I believe I saw froth of rage about her lips. She jerked the gold ring from her finger, and threw it far into the Lida River."

The sergeant paled. He remembered something from that morning at the steamer railing. "Your mother seems to have been a little intolerant in marriage?" he interjected.

"Fie... fie... sir!" Sara barked with blazing eyes and forgetting to say 'du'. "Albert?" she added immediately in a milder tone, "A twenty-times-kicked horse, which, on the twenty-first time kicks back, is not impatient. And that is certain and true before God," she said finally, with a barely noticeable, but deeply plaintive tone. "There was one person who constantly reminded, and proclaimed, that my mother would be all the better, or nobler, I think they call it, for all the suffering. But it was a lie. For, I know that she got worse, year by year. From the greatest orderliness and nicety, she became, in the end, ugly, hideous and shabby, and that it made me cry." (Sara began weeping.) "All the way from being a pious and godly person, she became, eventually, unable to even open a psalm book, and in the end... oh..."

"Pull yourself together."

"To this day, my mother is bedridden, and do you know from what? Lord have mercy upon us; drunkenness. That is not good for an old woman, Albert."

The sergeant stood up, felt a cold sweat under his uniform cap, took it off, and wiped his face with his handkerchief. In his mind, perhaps, some of his best plans were crushed at that moment. But, he was young, and did not have a hardened heart. He felt sympathy for his fellow human beings. Nor was he sufficiently sophomoric to come off with the usual false phrases: that bad was good. In the grips of shock and wonder, he found himself in a place where soldiers seldom approach. He sat down confidentially next to his suddenly open-hearted friend, and asked, "Tell me forthrightly, and strait out: are you what they usually call a 'Reader'?"

"A Reader... oh. Certainly not. There are a lot of those in West Gothland, but not me."

"Still, you read the scriptures, sometimes?"

"The Bible? Yes."

"You know, then, God's first, great commandment to all... forgive if this sounds a little... "Multiply, increase and fill the world." Shall that commandment not be fulfilled?"

After a little thought, but without difficulty, she answered, "All that about God's commandment does mean..."

"That a man and a woman should be together..."

"But that commandment does not mean that a man may be with just any woman in the world, I believe. And if a woman is together with whatever man she pleases, she will be afflicted with all sorts of circumstances and innuendoes. I want to remind you, that it says that a person shall be a help. That should not be one's downfall; neither the soul's nor body's downfall, but mostly the soul's. Except, just as one may detour, and get's out of the way of a great danger, accident, or suffering, and above all, to not have to associate with evil and dangerous company, then one should also avoid..."

At that moment a loud knocking was heard from forward in the steamer's foremast, and the captain and a machinist came running. It was, however, nothing worse than a hawser that had broken, and thereby the little sail was fluttering a little uselessly, and swinging back and forth in the wind. They had now come to one of Mälaren's larger watercourses, Granfjärden, where, with the transition to Blacken, the wind almost always blows freshly. The stronger rocking set all of the passengers in motion. The deck was filled with a crowd of faces that went unnoticed the day before, in the salon, but now crept out of their under-world like troglodytes. After a few minutes of fluttering, the sail was brought under control, and re-set to catch the wind properly. Everything calmed down, although the gale was not insignificant. But these ships, that travel with the strength of an inner fire, ask not much from wind or wave, but run their own straight path, whether the wind blows with or against, or, as now, from the side. In Granfjärden, there are many dangerous places; hidden rocks and reefs. They are the reason so many shipwrecks

33

have happened here, in the days of sailing without fire, and ships often had to tack into the wind. The ablest helmsman saw himself then, regardless of his knowledge of points and rocks, in the position of always avoiding them, because he had nothing in his disposal but the helm. He had nothing but those great, oversized, heavy, wind-cast sails that however he turned or tacked, still, often dashed off with him where he didn't want to go. A poor helmsman on a ship is, in any case, still not more than a man? Now that they drive their sails with fire, they go straight to their destinations, without tacking, and never using the sail more often than when the wind blew so that it drove them along. Now the helmsman still had to know the points and the reefs, of course; but with the knowledge of them, it was easy to avoid them, if he isn't an idiot. The only real danger in steam-sailing is destruction by fire, but even at that, the boilers can be constructed with safety measures, so that it seldom or never happens.

Then things happened quickly. The natural movement on deck meant that the sergeant and Sara were interrupted in their conversation about humanity's greatest problem. The sergeant, driven by his energetic nature, had run ahead, and grabbed at the sail, to the ship's captain's great joy, and appreciation. The result was a brother-Skål between them, below decks in the captain's quarters. This story will include exactly how a dinner time on a ship goes, for a deck-passenger has hardly any idea. He notices, merely, by the sun sinking toward the horizon, and the serving-girls hurrying with full cups of coffee, that dinner time on shipboard has come. The salon passengers had decided among themselves; and when some troglodyte-figures, a little happier than usual, or at least less ugly to the eye, appeared from their hiding place, then one of the people, (a foredeck passenger), can understand that the nobility were doing as usual. It is true, just as well, as this narrative has previously pointed out, that one or another of the deck men of bolder nature, can at least go down to the dining hall, and there have a quick bit, and then go up again. But the women of the people have it really difficult. How they live there on the bow of the deck has many times confounded historians. It doesn't seem proper that they bring food along, or feed themselves. And of the generally large amount of food that the steamship's galley cooks, they get none when they themselves have no more than deck-space. Perhaps among these women there is a bolder one, who goes down into the troglodyte's back-rooms and gets herself a goodie, and returns to the fresh air. But, that was not held to be too modestly done by her. It's good news now, with coffee, which is not food, but is good anyway at four or five o'clock. It came from the back-room, brought to the deck by young women, who, if they aren't feeling too unfriendly, allowed themselves to be spoken to, so that even a poor deck-person could get a cup. Sara took a chance and really became one: And she looked so proper and pretty, that, except for the shawl, the servers would likely take her for gentry. The truth was, unimaginably, that she, whose purse full of silver had caught several eyes, had not bought a salon ticket, and made a troglodyte of herself like the others. It must have come from her love of the open air, and distaste for the ugly smells, and salons in general.

While she drank her coffee, and was deciding whether to get another cup, she remembered with inner joy and gratitude Sergeant Albert's proposal to bring her ashore to the pleasant, red-painted little town (she had already forgotten the name). It was where she had had the opportunity, without any hassle, to have good meal, by the name of 'breakfast', although for her it was supper, and made it so that after she'd had her coffee, she felt well-fed, happy, and free. The sergeant had more devouring interests; and as this story had related previously, already a few times that morning, he had gone down and had persuaded the serving girls to help him in his need, and he was down there again. His new-found standing with the captain made it so that he could go up and down without difficulty, as much as he wanted, whenever he wanted, and one needed to look at his ticket to know that he, himself, did not belong to the aristocracy, but was of the people. Nothing was said about what, how, where, or when he ate; it was merely assumed that he would join for dinner. He was young, and had healthy needs, such as God creates; but he was in no way a gourmand, drinker, glutton, or slob, or otherwise a troglodyte. Neither did he seem comfortable in back-rooms, and left them as soon as possible, and must have been especially a friend of the air blowing from the bow, for he stayed there mostly, and now he lit his cigar again.

## Chapter Four

*He leaned sadly back in his chair, and laid his head against the arm-rest. You have no diamond, Albert! Close your eyes and sleep, and stick to your guns.*

Sara Videman surveyed her belongings, what she had in her bags on the foredeck. She seemed particularly concerned about one, for on one occasion, when no other person stood there on the foredeck, she took a chance, and patted the cigar-smoker on the arm, and said, "Is it okay if I ask you a little favor? I have a travel bag, that one with the brass S. V. Watch that no one sits on it! I have had it lying under the sail from the beginning, and all day, but the last time I had to leave it for a restroom break, they put the sail up, and now my bag is naked and bare."

Albert took the cigar from his mouth and said, "Is the bag so fragile that even a body as light as your own cannot sit on it?" Otherwise, that was the easiest way for him to guard it.

"No, no absolutely not. Neither I, nor you, and least of all anyone else."

"Is it full of diamonds?"

"Oh, now!"

"Well, what, then? Except, forgive me, it's none of my business. Be assured and happy, and go where you please. I will watch your bag."

Sara thanked him with a look, as if the bag were her own heart. She walked away to busy herself with the diverse boxes and cases that she set aside on the deck.

"What can she have in that luggage," thought Albert, as he stood looking at the shiny, gold 'S. V.', and drew a terribly long drag on his cigar. She's certainly a rich doll, anyway, no mistake. But, I don't care about that; I have enough money from (here he mumbled a mysterious family-name), and I get a percentage from the property in Vadsbo. The letters are nicely made. They have a pretty good brass foundry in Lidköping. Should I follow her all the way there? Otherwise, I'll have to get off at

37

Mariestad, and ride inland. Yeah. Let's see. It's a long way yet." "Hey, you, Miss! You with the tray! Bring me a new cigar: I don't want to get up from here. Damn! She didn't hear me! How did that happen? I don't want to smoke the butt any shorter. It tastes hot, and the smoke is getting in my nose, for crissake! The suitcases aren't big; fairly long, but not wide. She surely must have her glass boxes in there, because no one can sit on them. But who the hell would be so shameless as to sit on it? I've never seen the other deck-passengers sit on anything but the hawsers, or the pumps, or the cannons. They are pretty nice, polite people. They are so careful about other people's things that, for example, those Dala girls sat completely by themselves, that is they folded their legs underneath them. What shameless individual could Sara have feared would try to... aha... there, you see, Albert, she meant you, yourself, and no one else. When asked me so sweetly to watch her suitcase... shit, that tastes bad!" he said, and threw the cigar butt into the lake. This pushes my patience too far.

Just at this difficult juncture, Sara came to him and said to him, "What do you think?" and put a cigar in his hand. "I don't have a light with me," she said, "and I didn't want the waitress who sold it to me to light it for you down there, because... besides, she can't smoke, but how are you going to light it, Albe?"

"Well, look, here comes the captain strolling along, with one of his superb Trabucos in his yap. Excuse me, my dear captain sir... please step a few steps closer so I can get a light. This lovely young lady has assigned me to a post that I, as a good soldier cannot abandon."

"Aye aye!" answered the captain. Sara stood, and looked on, and could not help laughing out loud when the two men touched cigars, end to end, with serious, intent gazes upon the tips, working feverishly to ignite the cigar. They succeeded, and honorable captain walked cheerily on his way. With his own expression of satisfaction, the sergeant puffed his cheeks full of fresh, new smoke... for you know that the first drag tastes best...

and blew it out really slowly, but in his distraction, he blew it right in Sara's face.

"Oh!" she shouted, and ran away to the other side of the foredeck, where she had her previously-described luggage.

Once again, Albert stood, alone with his suitcase... which is to say her bag, and regarded the mild, lovely, westering sun. They had now come to Galten, the farthest part of Lake Mälaren on the way to Arboga. As previously said, Albert stood and looked at the sun, but he also sometimes looked at the bag. He smoked slower now, for he thought "If I smoke this cigar all at once, then it might not be as easy to get another one as before. Yes, surely she has glass in the bag, and I like that better than that she has glass in her breast, or that her whole heart was made of it, like I thought before. That was a dumb thought... puh!... but I shouldn't blow out so much smoke at one time... puh!... let it be that her soul is of glass just a little: can I not have a diamond as well as anyone? And cut? But not deeply. I don't have the heart to scratch into such beautiful crystal... puh!... I'll just scratch an "A" in the enamel of her mind. I can do that, can't I? That's not too much, is it? Puh!... She is beautiful when she is serious, but yet more beautiful when she smiles like that; and even more beautiful when she weeps for her mother. Strange that I should think of that. One usually looks ugly when they cry... puh!... but her eyes didn't turn red, they stayed as clear as... Well, she didn't weep long, anyway."

"Steer to leeward! Steer to leeward!" the captain shrieked to the coxswain. "Don't you see the buoy, you moron? Yes, okay, it's starting to get dark," added the captain good-naturedly. "It's best if I absolve him from steering, and do it myself. The channel to Arboga is not like the other easy passages. Steer to leeward! Leeward! Stop the engines, goddammit! Get out of here! I'll do it myself. Get the jib hauled in!"

"Stop the engines! Stop!" was heard in return. The ship slowed, and the skillful captain, standing at the helm himself, had time to correct course, and pass the buoy safely.

Mälaren's innermost waters, or the westernmost beginning outside Kungsbarkarö, and Björkskogs parishes, are full of small, shallow reefs, and on-shore dangers that one never encounters at sea. These little points of land closest to the Arboga River are a continuation of the low Kungsö fields, which, like a green carpet in the farthest west, seem intent on crawling in under the water. And, especially in the evening, one cannot see a clear division between the waves of grass, and the waves of the lake. Therefore, sailors sight in on the roof of Kungsö Castle, which lies not far from the mouth of the river. This time, as always, all went well for the Yngve Frey.

Just as they entered the river channel, a deep, dry voice up on the steamer's stern-deck said to his neighbor, "Now how far do we have to go, to get to the city?" "About nine miles," another voice answered, with a tone of greatest meekness, servility and eagerness. The voice was soprano like a woman's, without being one, as it was a man's. "Good," resumed the basso, and looked at his watch. "It's seven o'clock. We'll be there by eight or nine at the latest, and we can look forward to a proper table, and real beds." Words were exchanged between two family men. "If my baron commands," said the soprano, "It'll go easier, much easier, if we take the opportunity, as we pass Kungsö, to send a courier by land to the city to order a room for us. We'll run into a lot of people when we get there."

"Can that happen, Captain?" asked the basso politely, but indifferently. "It positively can, yes, for sure," interjected the soprano eagerly, before the steamship captain at the helm had time to answer.

"It can happen," said the captain, not without some awkwardness.

"How?" asked the basso, tired of so much talking.

"Yes, without difficulty, really quickly, altogether easy!" jumped in the soprano, with the quickest words in the world. The honorable captain at the helm looked around thoughtfully. "Yes, anyway," he said, "a boat could go ashore, and hire a fellow at the inn there to ride to the city, if it is so necessary. However, I hope to be there just as quickly."

"Oh yes, oh yes, oh yes," said the soprano. "We will make it to the docks just as quickly, with skillful captain's measures, but much time is then wasted, lost, taken away with disembarkation. So, it is always good –doesn't the baron wish it? – if we send a courier to rent all of the rooms?"

"See to it!" said the sleepy basso, and tucked his chin into his coat. The soprano bounced up like a happy greyhound, but bounced no farther than to the captain at the helm, who was quite close. "Order it, captain, order it, order it!"

The captain, as good-natured as he was, felt annoyed by all the toadying, but didn't want to do anything against the baron, so he shouted to one of his men. "Make the boat ready to go ashore and…" and he explained the errand. "You can row back to us after that."

"Yes, the baron will pay for your trouble, of course, of course, of course!" muttered the soprano, turning to the captain, and pointing at his boss, who was huddled into his coat.

"It is worth something," answered the captain easily, stroking his chin, and looking away to the two banks, between which he was steering. The view to the right side was broad, and captivating. The fields, in an immeasurable expanse to the north and west, lay covered with millions of hay-ricks, like the little unclipped knots on the back of a big, green tapestry.

"And Hörstadius has taken over all of this now? He is certainly a pastor!" said the captain with a nod, as he stood and talked to himself. Before he's dead, he'll be land-rich or land-poor. He's a pastor who preaches with hay. He can tell like it is in the scriptures: "All hay is meat; for, of these fields he brought it forth for this good purpose. Government authorities, or the Military… I don't really know… have been really good to him. But I wonder if he takes over property in other districts, not just here in Kungsör, but in Sörmland, too: yes, all over the whole kingdom. Doesn't he have lease-holdings all the goddam way up to Uppland, to Sollentuna? That's an economist, that

41

Hörstadius. And then he torments his poor body riding in farm wagons, and roaming around his entire life between his properties; to look after, and see to. It must be a hell of a lot of work to run a household in every part of the country. And all that dragging himself around like that, he gets so crosswise of his own body, that he only enjoys the water. Hörstadius is a West-Goth, therein lies the knot; they are a nation unto themselves. But what I like about him is that he is so upright and nice to all of his thousands of field-bosses, farm hands and inspectors, that in the end, he is said to vex no one more than himself. "Take in the sail! Raise the flag! No, a man who sails a steam boat is a minor martyr. Come here! Come and steer! I'm going below. Now the river is clear and easy to handle, all the way to Arboga."

The helmsman came at the command, and the captain handed him the helm, and walked across the deck to the companionway, and down to the lower quarters, where steaming toddy's were waiting. There was punsch, too. The sun's glow had already sunk westward into the embrace of Kungsör's fields, but a dark red-purple shimmer hung yet in the sky. It was the last feather boa that the beauty cast off before she lay down to slumber under the covers. Thousands of long red-blue streaks streamed out of the dimness, many of them striping the water, and some even lay splashed across the steamer's deck.

A soft hand touched Albert's shoulder. He looked up from the red streamers that he had long stood regarding, as they rippled and flowed above the water's surface. It was Sara, and she whispered, "Go now. I'll watch your stuff and mine for the rest of the trip, all the way until we come to land. Go down, and have a punsch. But when we get to the dock, you'll have to hurry up to the city, to get us porters before the other passengers get all of the porters."

They happened to be standing completely alone in the bow, so Sara did not need to whisper. But Albert thought it sounded so confidential and nice, and her pretty face was so close to his, that without realizing what he was doing, he kissed her, and then left, as she had told him. As if nothing had happened, Sara Videbeck began, to busy herself forward in bow, with greater and lesser urgencies. She set her own bags, chests, and coats together. She also carried the sergeant's not-very-extensive backpack, trunk and duster. You might ask how she recognized them, but the day's observations had been sufficient to notice which items the sergeant, in his wandering the deck, had paid special attention to, sometimes lifted, moved around, adjusted, etc, which a good fellow never does with any, but his own belongings.

Indeed, Albert went below, and had a glass of punsch. "Mamsell! Allow me to humbly ask for two more glasses, and put them on this little tray; I'll carry them myself, so that no one is inconvenienced." The waitress, pleased with such politeness from such a previously harsh traveler, quickly did as she was asked. Albert took his tray, formally as a waiter, up the companionway, and across to the bow to serve his travelling companion. "Is it Carolina?" she asked, "I don't drink punsch."

"Drink now, for my sake, this afternoon, it gets cool at night. It's fine, and smooth."

"Good!" she said, and then the glass was empty. "Albert, this is better than Carolina."

"That's what I've always said," answered the sergeant, and emptied the one standing next to it.

Now the cannon saluted the city of Arboga, and the steamer laid to on the high bank, as it usually did, below Lundborg's farm.

The sergeant, agile, lively, and in a first-class good mood, was the first to leap ashore. After a quick look around in the nearest street, he found a pair of idle Abogans, and soon came to an agreement with them. They followed him down to the steamer with a barrow they found in the neighborhood. Arriving back down at the ship, Albert was not finding the one he was looking for. A little surprised, he looked around in the twilight for that pink scarf... it was nowhere. However, in the end, he discovered; Sara Videbeck, wearing a hat. Although the two men with the barrow were waiting for instructions, he could not help standing for a few moments, to regard his transformed friend. Indeed, that morning he had had her right in front of him, for a few minutes, but he had looked at her without interest: "Now, is that her?" he thought. He did not at all want to regard her as a 'Mamsell', as she had warned him against. But that neat, white, cambric hat sat really nicely on that pretty, free, fine head; and a few tasteful dark locks hung down on each side at her temples, too. Albert pointed out to the two porters where to go. Sara said with the emphasis on the fourth word, "These things are *our* stuff. Be careful with them, that they aren't scraped up on the litter."

"No danger, fair lady," said the one man.

"Tell us yourself," remarked the other, "which ones the lady is most concerned about, and we'll put them on the top."

Albert smiled a little to himself, but saw a fairly sour, stern look on Sara's face. They came ashore. "Which way does the gov'nor command us to go?" asked the foremost bearer.

"To the inn."

"I see. The gov'nor doesn't live here in town? Then I might mention," continued the fellow, "that the gentleman should hurry to get quarters at the inn, for a lot of travelers have arrived."

"I'll follow with our things," interjected Sara, "Hurry ahead, Albert! We'll meet at the inn."

The sergeant complied. He traversed the long Arboga streets, and came, after a while to the inn.

"There are none! There are none!" was the innkeeper's answer to Albert's request for a room.

"But I've just come from the steamer and I need lodging."

"Well, if the gentleman came from the sun, or from Mount Olympus itself, there would still be no room. Here it is baron, and baron, and baron, who have taken all the rooms for themselves and their families. And as for the rest of Arboga, listen, I seriously doubt it. The market in…hmm... has created a frightful congregation."

"Well, I would be satisfied with a single room, (I, myself can sleep somewhere, he thought), but a nice one. It can be small. Please. The cost doesn't matter."

"Have you any single rooms left, Annette?" said the innkeeper, looking into a side room. There's a lot of damned nobility, who have completely taken up all our occupancy. We usually have enough room, but they all belong to the area's nobility, so you see..."

"No." answered Annette, "There's nothing."

"But, dammit, I must have a room," said the sergeant decisively. "All that's needed is a bed. It's impossible that there isn't one in such a big, spacious, beautiful hotel like this. I've been to Arboga before, and I know that long hallway along the courtyard leads to thousands of rooms."

"Now, now," said a little, short, round woman in a cap; the hotel's hostess. "Go, Annette, all the way to the end of the walk, and see if my own room can be scraped together into shape. In an emergency, I'll sacrifice my own comfort."

Annette and the sergeant left. He found a large, fairly decent room, gave his approval, and returned to the office. He had hardly reached the portal, when he met Sara and the porters. He showed them the way up the stairs to the long hallway, paved with boards, and which, like a loft or an arcade, stretched the length of the floor. The walk had put a healthy glow on Sara's cheeks, and she was feeling cheerier. The sunniness was quickly overcast with a cloud of stern disapproval at the porter's polite invitation, "You first, pretty lady!"

She quickly regained her composure, and, followed by Albert and Annette, walked into the room, which she found charming. Quickly, cheerily, she organized their things along one wall of the room. The porters were paid, and dismissed. After Annette told them about the little room below, that had been cleared for dining; the two of them walked down, and enjoyed a simple evening meal, which Sara Videbeck, in particular, could really use.

A half hour passed, and then they walked back up from the dining room. Annette walked ahead, to open the door to the room.

"God, I hope you gentle-folk are pleased!" said Annette. We don't have any better for the travelers. I'll come right back with candles." With a curtsey, she walked out, and left them alone together.

The broad, nicely made bed gave testimony to what the good-natured Annette took them to be. Albert, in order to immediately prevent any awkwardness, said, "Dear Sarah, I'll sit in the carriage, down below, or spend the night in a hayloft. That person's ignorant assumption about you annoys me as much as you, but I didn't count on greedy barons taking all of the rooms; that I could only secure one, and that on a hardship basis. On the other hand, I hope that you shall be comfortable here, remain undisturbed, and sleep well."

All this time, Sara took off her hat, laid it on the chair, and walked over to her travelling companion with a friendly bearing, and answered, "Do as you will, and sit outside wherever you please, Albert. I can well imagine that you would make a fuss, and think it's dumb, that there's only one nice, decent, room. You wouldn't talk so much of this triviality, if you had been born, raised, and spent your entire life in just a single room, as I did; a room that in the daytime was a workshop, and at night was a bedroom for us all together. (The other rooms in the house had to be rented out). But, although you aren't like all the others, I can still see that you were raised with a lot of foolish ideas. Therefore, good Albert... yes, do as you please, but I can assure you, that if you remain here, instead of sitting out there in the weather all night, I won't think anything of it, and I wish you would see it that way, too, for then it will matter even less.

"If you stay in here, I won't think anything of it!" echoed in the sergeants soul, and something so crushing for his self-confidence, so cruel, and humiliating, struck him dumb.

"Albert!..." she continued, stepping close and taking his hand, "Don't mistake me, and don't wonder. Long ago, when Papa was still alive, he mostly stayed out, but sometimes he came home anyway, with a lot of commotion, fights, trouble, and cursing that went on until four in the morning. But I can assure

46

you that otherwise it was so still in our workshop where we slept, that not the least glass was broken. That's what I was used to. But go ahead, and go out, dear Albert, for perhaps you see too much in this little matter, and I cannot change you."

Now he had to smile. It couldn't be helped. He released her hand. "Just as well," he answered. Now I'll at least go out, and order us some horses for tomorrow."

"Of course. You should go now. Yes," interjected Sara hastily, "tomorrow it'll be too late to make arrangements. We must be ready early. And, wherever it is that you'll be sleeping tonight, please take the room key with you, so that no one else comes in by mistake. Also, tell the maid not to bring candles up. I can see well enough to go to bed."

Albert left. He turned around at the door. She stood in the middle of the floor, and curtseyed. "Good night, Albert. We'll see each other in the morning!"

He bowed, closed the door, and removed the key. "Incomprehensible!" he said between his teeth. "Good night! I'll see you first in the morning! Is that an invitation to come back in the afternoon?"

"And, is that what she meant in the first place, anyway? I'm going to take the battle down to the yard."

He concluded the business of ordering horses down below, and told Annette that no candles were needed, but that coffee should be brought in at exactly six a.m. Then he walked around the yard looking for wagons, and for a place to sleep, but none were to be seen. Noticing some standing thistle-stalks, he found cracks in the shed, that gave him access to the diverse coaches of the gentry, but they were all locked. He walked down to the sloping yard. The night looked like it would rain. He came to the stable, and knocked on the door. From inside a stable-lackey shouted drunkenly, "Go to Hälsingland!"

[Hälsingland is a province of Sweden and also a euphemism for Hell. Trans.]

"It's a fine horse's ass of an innkeeper, who so early and proper, closed all his sheds, gates, and barns!"

47

"Congrats, sergeant! You'll have some quiet here. Shut off from the whole of humanity."

"I'm going back up for a minute, to see if Sara is keeping a smile on her face, and if she'll let me see her. Then I'll come back down, and make a place for myself, with such a sanctified Hälsingland stable-boy."

Curiosity drove him to the first part. Still, he paced back and forth across the angular stone paved yard, during which he clicked his heels, and talked to himself. "'Good night!' she said. That is true. But her voice trembled a little, then. I noticed that. Sweetly, inscrutably, as if from the heart. It can be explained as one pleases, and a decisive 'good night' need not mean a dismissal. It could be the other way around. I'd like to put her to the test; nettle her, and not go up. 'I'll see you in the morning!', as in, 'not tonight?' Hadn't it been left to my own choice to decide which I wanted? I'll just see about her. I'll go up in a minute; a half minute."

He slowly climbed the stairs, walked the length of the long walkway, carefully put the key into the lock, opened, and walked in. It was silent in the room. He approached in the half-darkness. Sara's clothes lay on a chair, where she had taken them off, and folded them neatly. She herself? He stretched his neck to see. She was already asleep, with her face turned to the wall. Albert's first reaction was a cool rapture; for, without being a poet, much less zealously religious, but rather purely, and simply a sergeant, he was struck irresistibly by such great, simple freedom; such pure, and unseen virtue. Without knowing if he would return or not, she had gone to bed, safe and sound, and immediately gone to sleep, without inner uproar, without trepidation, without verses, without stories.

But Albert's next thought was not as pleasant. He found that it certainly had been her cool and complete seriousness, when she expressed that it mattered not at all, if he stayed in the room. What then did he mean to her? The same as a chair… a table… a doorpost, all the same.

48

Crushing! Devastating! The most beautiful girl allows, without difficulty, a chair to be present at her toilet. Pretty flattering to enjoy the same indulgence!

Albert pulled off his boots; walked silently and crestfallen a turn across the floor, took off his coat, and because he had just been fantasizing about chairs, he looked for one, and found one with armrests and a huge backrest. It was one of those historical chairs that have been in castles and small towns since the sixteen hundreds, where they had come through the auctions' world-wide dominion.

He quietly carried the chair over to a window, sat down, and gazed out through the window-panes at the night sky, and tried to sleep. However, he couldn't even yawn. His chair was soft, but he felt prickly in his chest, and the whole room stood in cold, dark misery around him. He looked toward the bed. It gleamed white from the clean, freshly ironed pillowcases. Besides that, it was dead and meaningless.

For something to do, he sat for a while with his eyes closed. But, he could still see. What did he see? A long arabesque unrolled before his inner vision. There appeared all of the special, little events of the past day, and Sara's image renewed constantly; but so mild, so happy. It was, at first, the moment in Strängnäs, when they became 'du'; and when she came with the cigar, etc. "Is it possible that after all this that she hates you?" he asked himself.

"Stupid sergeant!" he said half aloud, and stared up at the ceiling. "Hate me? That she certainly does not. Does one hate a chair? Does one hate a table? Hate a piece of furniture? An indifferent... a nothing... a me!"

He listened to discover if her sleep wasn't troubled, in some way. But, there was no sign of that. "Sara Videbeck is not of those who dream," he sighed, and shut his eyes. "In the end, she has a glass heart, anyway: hard and cold, shiny but hard. Certainly, she neither asks for hate, nor love. But what does that make her? She herself is like a chair, without feeling. As if she held me for a chair, and said so open-heartedly. Virtuous? Can I call chair virtuous? She is nothing at all like that, as I see it. Neither good nor evil. How can I call a nothing 'virtuous'? Or even given to vice? But pardon me, Sergeant, you are incorrect," he continued, after a pause, "She is not, as you say, a nothing at all like that. Do you remember, for example, those lively glances, the warm mouth? Then, and then... no, she has feelings, well enough, be certain of that. But if I am right, see, there is another question. What is she, then? A wanton? To Hälsingland with that! I can't go along with that. But she's a middle-thing that I won't understand if I burst my temples trying. I want to be a poet again. I'm only twenty-five years old."

"Oh!" he continued, "If I could only sleep. Tomorrow it will be okay." However, in spite of his wish, he looked out through the window, instead, and up at the firmament, which had cleared, and showed some stars now. He rubbed his hand on the pane to clear the fog. "What is a pane of glass," he began to monologize, "What is a glass pane, here in the world? It is a middle thing, too. A thing between 'in' and 'out'; wonderfully enough. For the window-pane itself, isn't seen, but still decisively separates the little human world, from the immeasurably great 'out'. I can see nothing in the pane of glass, but through it I can see the heaven's stars. The window-pane is insignificant, perhaps even humble; still, it is not just a low being, I don't think, but neither of high value. Yes, for example, like myself! Oh, I want so badly to scratch my name in that window-pane. I have only a flint in my vest pocket. If she spoke truly, when she said that glass could not be cut with it, I'd still like to try."

He pulled it out and tried. But, either the flint was too dull, or he didn't want to make any noise with greater exertion, in a word, he could not scratch a mark. Then he leaned back sadly in his chair, and laid his head against the armrest. You are without a diamond, Albert. Close your eyes and sleep. And fold up your pretentions!" His inner vision grew ever dimmer, the figures ever duller and greyer. His pulse beat without heat; his heart beat quite slowly, and softly. The universe was quite sad. He slept.

## Chapter Five

*I mean, there will still be very much that we may thank each other for, that no money can repay.*

In the morning, there was a gentle tapping on the door. Albert sat up in his chair, and there was even a small, detectable stirring of the covers on the bed. The key that had been left in the lock outside turned nicely once around, the door opened, and in walked Annette with a coffee tray.

"Please forgive me for being late with the coffee, sweet gentlefolk," she said, chattily and familiarly, as the help in small town hotels sometimes happen to be. The gentleman is already up, I see. Sorry! I know that travelers would rather have their coffee in bed, but God knows how it's been today. It's already seven thirty. All those barons kept us on the go until late last night, getting everything just the way they wanted it. God! Stick a fork in it, and let it be done!"

Sara raised her head, and sat up against the pillow. Annette went over to the bed, curtsied, and turned the breadbasket to offer the beautiful rusks, gleaming inside, for the "sweet lady" to choose.

In the meantime, Albert had pulled on his boots. A barely perceptible nod from Sara constituted a silent "good morning". The glow of her happy, new-wakened face was a refreshing waker-upper for him. He thought he caught a glimpse of a wave, and went over and sat on the broad edge of the bed, where the unused covers were tucked in through the night. Now Annette offered him his coffee. He took it, and tasted it.

"Do the gentle-folk need anything more?" she asked at the door.

"Why not?" said Albert. She left.

After a few moments of awkwardness, he remarked, "Dear Sara, I realize that you are annoyed at the false titles people give you and me, quite correctly, but during this journey we would be spared a lot of dreary innuendo and stupidity, if this one time… or…"

"I have realized the same thing," she answered, "and I'm not angry. I would in no way spread an untruth, but it did so on its own, so...and... Albert, I'm really glad that you didn't misunderstand me, or misperceive just now, when I waved for you to come, and sit down on that part of the bed. It's a strange, terribly wide bed. I slept like a queen... but I didn't want the girl to notice that that part of the bed was unused. She would get strange thoughts about us."

Albert put on his coat, approached the door, and said, "I'll go down and see about the horses."

He did so. The horses that he had ordered had come along with a buggy, the whole bottom full with hay and straw, and two seats consisting of two ordinary hard farmer's seats. "She won't like this farm-style stuff. I know that. The innkeeper will have to lend me a seat with a cushion," he said to himself.

He went, and after a period of negotiation, he got one. It was tied down to the front of the wagon with new lead-ropes. "But," thought Albert, "Right here over the axle between the front wheels, it shakes something terrible. It's better if the farmer sits there and drives, and we sit in the back in the middle between the axles. Otherwise, I'd just as soon sit in front and drive, but God knows if she will approve of having the horses tail so close; almost right at one's feet. In particular when they go downhill, l and the horses hold back, and you have them all the way to your knees. Such things amuse me, but she, I think surely, would not be happy with such countrified foolishness. I'll go up, and ask where she wants to sit."

Perhaps here, the sergeant's polite thoughtfulness went so far as childishness. Meanwhile, he bounced lithely, and happy up the steps, reached the door, opened the lock, and walked in. Sara was already standing there, dressed and ready, from top to toe. She had not put on her hat, and the six-hands-long braid had not been twirled up into its loops to lie above her neck in a comb.

"Now, a proper 'good morning,'" she said. "We had not actually greeted each other. I've seen through the window, that the

wagon has arrived. But," she added with mild, gentle, slightly wavering voice, "You had an uncomfortable night for my sake?"
In her appearance, as she stood there, lay an expression of great thankfulness, along with the pleasure of unlimited trust in his person. And still, she had an added expression of not-so-little female humor.

Albert didn't answer. It was impossible for him at that moment not to do what he did. He swept her into his arms, and kissed her.

Afterwards, Sara Videbeck went immediately to their luggage to see how it should be loaded into the wagon for it to ride properly. When Albert stood in the door to go fetch the farmhand who would carry their things down to the wagon, she waved him back and said, "I have come to a decision about something. It is best if you alone sign the registers, and pay drivers on this trip, for the drivers can seldom add, and it makes me so mad when I have to deal with them, that I lose my good humor. But here is my part of the travel expenses from here to Mariestad; one horse for me at twenty-four shillings per mile for fifteen and a half miles makes seven riksdalars, thirty-six crowns. Wagon rental is forty-six and a half crowns. Transportation from the cities of Arboga and Örebo (we can't do more cities) and lodging, altogether eleven riksdalars, six crowns. Look, I don't think I calculated hastily. I'm used to it, and I'm quite capable. Still, count it over, yourself."

Humiliated, and with lowered head, the sergeant did not answer, but put out his hand to receive the silver coins rolling out of her purse.

"Sweet Albert," she added sadly, "Perhaps I was mistaken and you are not going as far as Mariestad? I thought you said yesterday sometime, that you were going to Vadsbo parish, and as far down as Mariestad. I figured our mutual travel expenses to there. If I am wrong, please tell me."

"I wasn't brooding about that," he answered, "But I can't deny that I would have liked to have paid for the whole damn expense myself, as I am not exactly ready for the poor-house. And when we part company, we could always settle up then… and…"

Sara looked at him wide-eyed. "Yes. So." She said, at last, and turned her half-sad gaze a little to the side. "No, Albert. Don't talk so much. All the settling up afterward is awkward for people who like each other. It will be just as awkward for you then, as now, to accept my share; and I would feel even more awkward, I'd be sitting on pins and needles, that in the end, I would not have a chance to give it. To be beholden like that is unbearable."

"My God, Sara, Are then mutual favors… is… yes… gratitude between two human hearts such an unbearable feeling?"

"Gratitude… Albert! (At this, her eyes raised prettily) There are things that one can never lay aside: Thankfulness is nice, then. To stand in eternal debt to someone is lovely. But travel expenses, and money for food, and lodging, and pleasure; some may want to be indebted for those, but not I. And I understand that if I had no money, then I would go ahead, and accept. I would be shamed and humbled, and I would thank you, weeping. But to avoid that, I intend to never get lazy about it. And, as far as possible, I think I'll take care of my own requirements. Don't talk about it. Take the money in your hand, Albert, and be a real fellow! Oh… there will probably still be much, much more that we will have to thank each other heartily for, I think, that no money can repay."

The tear that was now hanging on the tips of her long, dark eyelashes did not fall, but slowly drew back into her eye. Thus, without falling, it merely increased the gleam of her eyes, and they shone unworldly.

Albert began to understand that it was not at all a low deed to accept the money. He took it, yes; he even went so far as to count it carefully, as if taking it from a peddler. He found the sum to be correct, and said coldly, and decidedly, "You have counted correctly, Sara."

She understood the victory that he had won over himself, and rewarded it with her own nod. "I knew that, but it does not hurt to have two add it up; it always works out better. With that, she took her long braid, and twirled it neatly under the comb at her neck, put on her hat and, went toward the door.

The sergeant forgot to ask about the seating arrangement. They came down to the courtyard, and told the driver to go up and get their things. He went, and came back down with their luggage, one after another, which Sara arranged in the long wagon, while Albert went to the innkeeper, paid, and signed the register.

"We usually need to see your travel documents," said the innkeeper, "But it won't be necessary for you gentlefolk."

"Yes, of course. Look here, if it is required." Albert unfolded his documents for him to see.

He read: "Serg…Serg…yes, this is all very good. Your wife is not mentioned here, but it does not matter. It's all fine."

"Yes, my dear host." interjected Albert, "To tell the truth, when I got my papers, I intended to travel alone. However, as you know, often one can change his mind, and I brought her along, afterward, but I didn't want to trouble the police with issuing new papers."

"Well, I understand. What does it matter, then? One never asks for documents from proper folk, traveling respectably, and paying their way. Bon voyage, Mr. Sergeant. I hope you gentlefolk will be pleased with the horses. They are my own."

"Okay, Mr. Innkeeper. Now, if I can hand over the fare to Fellingsbro, we are finished."

"No, that's not necessary, although you might go ahead and pay, as the driver drinks."

"Look, seven and a half miles… and a little more. Where did Annette go? Please take this for what I owe her."

"My humble thanks. I'd like to offer a glass, Mr. Sergeant, on the house! A little nip in the morning can't hurt anything. Tell me, shouldn't I offer the lady out there a glass? I have a fine Malaga."

"I'm afraid that Sara will decline, this early in the day."

"You'll have to get used to that. First rate! I'll bet the lady is from West Gothland. The sergeant has made an excellent

57

choice. Now, I really hope the wagon is in good shape, and doesn't shake too much, but when you don't have your own transportation, you have to be happy with what you get. I, myself married a girl from West-Gothland, where you find the best folk. Perhaps I should not mention it, but I am related to someone who is related to Hörstadius himself. I have seen Mr. Sergeant before; a tall, good-looking, stately fellow! And I hope to get to…on your return trip… Your humble servant… humble servant…"

The sergeant could not refuse the drink, but the innkeeper's almost fatherly devotion, and confidentiality surprised him a little, and reminded clearly him of his position as under-officer.

Arriving out in the yard, he saw Sara already sitting on the wagon seat. The host came along with a glass on a tray. "Permit me! Permit me!" he murmured.

But Sara turned her head away, and said testily, half-aloud, "I don't waste my time on that; particularly not in the morning."

Albert felt a certain sting, said nothing, but took the reins and whip, and climbed up onto the seat. He drove out through the inn's gate, and absent-mindedly started driving fast.

"Oh! Look now! Look now! This is not acceptable!" she shouted.

The sergeant was irked, as he gave himself credit for driving really well. He jerked at the horses reins, cracked the whip, drove out through the gate, and away through the streets of Arboga to the western gate, so that it made the cobblestones smoke. You can imagine how the wagon, all the while, shook and bounced. "Drive friendly, good sir!" said the farmhand, sitting on the seat behind, reminding him, half rising. "Remember your place, you oaf, sit down and shut up!" shouted the sergeant.

They had now come to the main road. Even and well made, it permitted fairly high speed without anyone feeling abused. The farm-hand kept silent, and took a nap, since it wasn't his own horses. Sara had sat surprised ever since the gate and cast fearful glances to the right, to see if Albert were really angry.

58

When the sergeant drove horses, he would become so absorbed in the pleasure, that he neither saw nor heard anything else. For a half hour; a whole hour, not a single word was spoken.

At one point Sara said, "It's dusty!" That fact was irrefutable, and there was nothing to be done about it.

After a while, Sara said again, "The dust is too damned much. I think I'll take off my hat."

Meanwhile, the sergeant had pretty much regained his aplomb, so that he did not answer what she said, but asked, "Would you rather sit in the back seat? I see that the pale horse is constantly whipping at your shoes with his long, unclipped tail."

"I don't have a problem with that. He's dusting them off."

"Well, that's fine. Then you don't care to sit in back?"

"Next to the farmhand? So now you don't have room to drive here on the front seat?"

"Okay. But the farmhand could sit here, and drive, and both of us sit in the back. It would not shake you so much, Sara."

"I can't say that it shakes so much. It was a lot worse on the streets of Arboga."

"But if you take your hat off, for the dust, as you say, what good will that do? There won't be less dust."

"No, but a white cambric hat that gets all dusty must be washed immediately, and that's a lot of trouble, for it must be washed in the lake with a brush. On the other hand, the dust comes right off of a silk shawl if one slaps it a few times with the hand."

"Okay. If you want to change hats, I'll stop right now, and we can get down from the wagon."

"Or if I open the umbrella, and hold it against the dust?"

"The dust isn't like rain," interrupted the sergeant, "falling down from above down onto the umbrella. The dust rises up from below, and, unfortunately, swirls around your head. I don't like umbrellas in nice weather."

Sara fell silent. They traveled another fifteen minutes without conversation. At that point the farmhand woke up, and thrashed around so much, that it was like a revolution in the back of the wagon.

59

"What is he doing with our stuff?" Sara shrieked, turning her head. Albert slowed the horses and looked around. It was nothing worse, than that the farmhand had rolled over onto his left side to continue his nap.

With this, Albert shook off his foul mood, laughing at the grotesque position the sleeping Arbogan had taken, under his crumpled hat. He said, "You know, Sara Videbeck, now that we've stopped, I think we'll wait here for a bit. The horses can catch their breath; we've been driving fast. Meanwhile, you can make whatever changes you like, for the dust."

He jumped down, and walked around the wagon, and gave his traveling companion a hand to help her down. She stood up, but took a long time fumbling for a foothold with her shiny boot-toe. The wheel hub seemed to her to be too greasy to step on. The sergeant thought she was taking too long, so he let go of her hand, and instead, picked her up, lifted her to the ground, and said, "Now you'll see that you've been riding so long that you are unaccustomed to standing."

"I feel just fine, and can stand well enough, I think. But, you were driving awfully fast, Albert, in particular on… You know the magistrate in Lidköping has placed a ban on travelers driving through the streets as if they are going to a fire."

"The magistrate is stupid, Sara. I'll have to watch out when I am traveling to Lidköping. But honestly, aren't you thirsty in this dog's-foot dust? I know of a little spring up on this hill. Don't you think this district is really pretty?"

"This is a district? Is it far to Fellingsbro?"

"But, have you no love for beautiful landscapes?"

"Landscapes?" she asked, looking around indifferently. "They are so seldom painted naturally, Albert. Mama had a couple of landscapes hanging on the walls at home in the shop, ever since Papa's time. I had them carried up to the attic."

"I see. But don't you find this to be a real view? Look off there, farthest to the west lies beautiful Frötuna; formerly Dalson's, now it is Count Hermanson's property."

"I think we have a view in every direction I turn. But tell me, isn't this a parish? We always have parishes as soon as one leaves the city. And every parish has its master craftsmen in shoemaking, and tailoring, who have apprentices, not journeymen. I am glad that the parishes haven't gone so far as to have their own glass-masters yet, at least, so far as I know, not in the parishes around Lidköping. I know that I've had to go out to Råda, Åsaka, Gröslunda, Sävared, Linderva, Hovby, Trassberg, and even out to Skallmeja, to do installations."

All this time the sergeant stood in front by the horses, murmuring to them, for it seemed impossible for him to engage this beautiful woman in a sensible conversation on the beauty of the area. In her defense, it should be admitted that the area between Arboga and Fellingsbro is not exaggeratedly beautiful.

"What road did you travel to Stockholm, Sara?" he asked after a while, when she had stored her hat in a sturdy box, and in its place put a beautiful, long, shiny light grey silk scarf on her head.

"Going there?"

"Yes, Sara. Did you go the same way to Stockholm as we are traveling now? I think you are somewhat indifferent about the road and the surroundings here."

"I bought a ticket on the Thunberg," she answered, "I boarded it outside Kållandsö, on its way from Vänersborg. Then we sailed here and there, until we came to Stockholm's docks at Riddarholme."

"But, ever since we were in Arboga I thought that you were acquainted with the inns and the cities that we are passing, and along this route."

"Of course I would know about them, since I had intended to go this way on the return trip, because I had business to take care of in Örebro and Hova. I'm going to sell some mirror-goods to Selin. It could pay for the trip. And there is no great art to getting information on lodging. Look, and you shall see, Albert. I have made a list of all of the places, and mileage, that I drew up at Warodel's shop in Stockholm, from the information I got there. I read the list over completely before I went to sleep last night."

Albert looked at the list and found a fairly legible, feminine, hand style. "And she lay there and committed it to memory before she went to sleep last night, just as I was... (A crushing thought went through Albert).You truly did not busy yourself with any interesting subject before you went to sleep," he said aloud, with a sour expression.

"I read the whole thing through; distances and names. It wasn't too bad. Then I figured up my part of the transportation, so I would know how much I ought to give you in the morning before we left. It was fun; I thought about all the while, and fell right to sleep and slept well."

"Right. That last part was just the subject to put you to sleep," Albert remarked. The horses had now sufficiently caught their breath, and the sergeant, not in the best of moods, at least irked at people's sleeping ability, walked over to the driver, and woke him with a sharp poke. "Hans, Mikel, or Bastard, whatever you are called, should you be sleeping when you're supposed to be driving the passengers? Get your butt up, and out of the seat!

The driver, groggy from sleep and surprised at gruff, strict voice, scuttled down from the wagon, obediently and slavishly, as servants in the cities often are. "What's going on?" he asked.

"Tie the reins here, and change seats. Put your stool in the front, sit down, and drive. The road to Fellingsbro is so nice and even now, that the biggest bovine could drive it. I only enjoy driving when it is windy, and difficult. So, let's pick up the pace I say, you sleepy rotter! And fasten this upholstered seat in the back, in the middle of the wagon, and let's get going again."

The driver eventually regained his gallantry, and promptly carried out "Mr. Ossifer's" orders. Sara Videbeck did not say a word during this exchange, but she did smile a little at some of the jibes.

They climbed up and sat on the seat in its new position. The farm-hand was driving now, and the activity put him in an excellent mood. Wanting to show his good cheer, he cracked the whip, and drove like the Devil himself, to use the poet's expression.

The whip-cracking brought them to Fellingsbro. "Look what big, beautiful, red-brown houses!" were Sara's first words after the long silence. Presumably, she meant the two Fellingsbro Buildings, with their gable ends toward the road, standing so symmetrically with the spacious, square, clean courtyards between them, and the garden in the background, screened from the peasants, and freight-wagons, by a fence along the road.

Albert did not answer her outcry over the houses, but stepped down, settled up with the driver, and got horses for the trip to Glanshammar, as well as an equally good wagon and seats.

Once again they climbed up and sat. The new driver, a brown, wrinkled, but spritely old man would drive the horses himself, and that was no loss, as he tore off down the road fairly briskly. After a while, he turned the wagon to the left, south, and they entered the forest. The old man talked to his horses uninterruptedly, in a gruff, muttering voice which, although not Swedish, they were able to understand. It is just as well not to try to repeat it here. Happy to handle them alone, he neither saw nor heard anything else but the road, and them.

## Chapter Six

*"What, is she shivering?" thought Albert. "Well, God be praised! Then she is, after all…" "Why are you shivering, Sara?" he said aloud.*

"How I love this forest, Albert!" said his traveling companion, as they continued the ride away from Fellingsbro, and into Käglan Forest. The words were uttered in an almost caressing tone. She probably thought it was sad to go for so long without close companionship. The sergeant looked at her, and thought, "Yet, does she seem to have a mind for this beautiful country?" So, half-mollified, he said… No, he said nothing, but he was, however, dying to speak.

With a yet warmer, and more caressing voice she added, after a few minutes, "For here one has shade from the sun, and is spared from the dust!"

"So… that's all?" thought the sergeant, becoming completely sullen.

Sara Videbeck pulled her gloves off, as her fingers were feeling sweaty. She folded them up, and stuffed them into her hat. There-upon, she began to wave her two plump, white, dimpled hands up and down in the air to cool them.

After a while, Albert said mildly, but a little strangely, as if he were waking up from something, "Tell me, my best, good Sara, does it ever happen that you dream at night?"

"Oh yes, it happens."

"But it's probably been very long ago? Maybe you haven't dreamed since you were a little child?"

"Me? I dreamed in Arboga last night."

"Ah! Well, I wouldn't know that."

Sara held her hands still. She let them lie on her knees clasped together. "I cannot speak of my dream," she said in a low voice, "But it is a really beautiful dream."

Albert interjected, "I, for my part, did not dream after I fell asleep last night, but I did before."

"Oh, I could never believe that. However," she interrupted herself, everybody dreams in his own way. And that is probably for the best, too."

The sergeant took one of her hands. "When you dreamed at night, did you have your hands clasped like this?"

"I don't remember where I had my hands. But, I do remember, though." She added quietly, almost inwardly.

"Did you not, at least, dream that you were in a forest somewhere? I'd bet on that. And not that you were in the countryside, either…"

"And not that I was on a lake, either, Albert! No, I dreamed that I was in a little, tiny room with pink wallpaper and that I was grinding chalk…"

"Bah!"

"And the same to you, Albert. I can very well talk about it, (she continued in the same tone without paying notice to his nose-wrinkling). I dreamed a lot about you."

"And was I grinding chalk, too?"

She looked up at him with a big, warm glance, but looked away, as if met by a mist. She swallowed imperceptibly, and started to cry, pulled herself together and said, "It's just that I understand, Albert, you are an officer. Still, I had hoped that you would be more of a non-com than you actually are."

These words were pure Greek to the sergeant, and the wondering look he gave her, told her well enough that she was speaking incomprehensibilities. She drew her hand back from his.

"So, one can dream," she said, seemingly mostly to herself, "And when one awakens, everything is different. Therefore it is best that each and every one lives free by himself, in his own way, and not ruin things for each other. People can still be good friends, and that is best. It's all the nicest when it's good, and one doesn't cause trouble for those closest to him."

Albert wrinkled his forehead. "She's talking about her dream," he thought. Meanwhile, she continued:

"And God knows best, how he wants people to be, but doesn't understand the individual identity, the 'I'. Still, it is best to live as God created us."

These broad words fell on the sergeant's ears as so ridiculous, that he was on his way to a belly-laugh. But in respect for the expression in the girl's face, that looked so very thoughtful, he restrained himself, and tried to follow her train of thought.

"I must have an enlightenment from Sara Videbeck," he said. "Your mother lived an unhappy life with your father. I heard that from what you said yesterday, but don't believe that because of that, all evil comes from men…"

"I know that very well," she answered. "Indeed, I know master-turner Stenbergs. His wife is such a difficult battle-ax, that the poor fellow may lose his liver for her sake. And it's no better with the Sederboms, where the wife is so picky; the fellow is going crazy with misery. And the Spolanders, then. And the Zakrissons? It's the same everywhere, just get close enough, and see them in their cages. It doesn't stop until they have made complete wretches of each other. I could never go for that."

"Your father, Sara, was he so mean to your mother from the beginning?"

"God only knows. I was not born then, and didn't see them at first. But my mother, poor dear, always conducted herself in a certain way, I understand, despite the way she worked by herself... In the beginning, she was very orderly, I truly believe. But, just the same, she became slovenly and difficult. And her ways were never too sweet, or even just plain nice, I don't think. So that Father, who, again, had his own ways, eventually became like that, and in the end, evil, and completely ridiculous... Usch!"

"This is getting too troubling, dear Sara. Let Lidköping be as it is. We are not there, yet. Do you know the name of this forest?"

"Yes, I think God forgives me; that I am as he created me. That is, in my best way, of course. But that I should torment someone all the way into hell, or that someone should drive me there, is unnecessary. What is this forest called, Albert? I don't care at all. But I do know that God created all of the stars, and all of the sky. And everything that is beautiful and good that stands on earth; God made it. And Christ has come to our salvation. Although I am not a lay reader, I can well understand that Christ has nothing against people holding each other in a beautiful way, and fulfilling God's first commandment. But that it should go on in a way that they make devils or fools of each other, He Himself must not like that. But people find so much stupid material for each other's nastiness. And worst of all, is when they get it into their heads that it is of use to them. As far as you are concerned, Albert, you are younger, as a man, than I am as a woman, even if you are a year or two older than I am, as humans are counted. Therefore, you are not as wise as me, and I know more. However, you know other things that are happier, and more beautiful. Still, you should not believe that I am tired of myself. I am as light, and carefree as a bird. And you can be sure that I think I'll always keep my wings. If you can fly too, that is good. But if you're just a smooth talker, say so right now."

A big, grandiose pause.

"You can get offended and angry," continued the glass-master's daughter, "I have seen that, and that will just have to be, as long as you become angry over real things. Except, (she added in a low voice), it's impossible to calculate in advance, or predict. I've seen and experienced enough to know that. That which hardly scratched the fingernail of one, tears at the heartstrings of another and burns like a poison. God knows best how he wants people, but I don't get it."

The sergeant felt like he had quickly aged twenty years older than he was a little while ago, and he said, "Now Sara shall hear what I am all about. I am not a master-craftsman. But you don't value that, in terms of household relationships, if I can judge from what you've said about your father, and the other elders in Lidköping. Nor am I an officer, who, according to your choice of words, is either a lay-about or a smooth talker; at least not in the larger sense. So, I am an under-officer, plain and simple. What was done that I liked so much about you yesterday, I really cannot remember. And, I am afraid the story of it would not

68

sound factual enough for you. You... as far as your spunky way of talking is concerned, and your didacticism... you are about as West-Goth as you can be. But I, myself, am crazy enough, that I don't think the less of you for it. Without a doubt, you should ask me who I am, and where I was born. You haven't asked me, and I must admit that that indifference has wounded me a little. But we are long past talking about little hurts. Therefore, I want to tell you straight out, that I don't have any big wings to fly with, but I'm not completely lacking in feathers. My service to the crown is insignificant, however, through it I have the right to the uniform, and exercise has brought discipline to the body. That is what a man needs most, and unless he is a stupid, useless dog, he will, thereby, go as far in the world as he wishes. For, to learn knowledge, that is an easy thing for those who wish to, but discipline and manners are more difficult, and I don't want to go farther for an example of that than you, yourself, Sara. You don't seem to have had a lot of education, aside from the schooling you got in the work-shop. None-the-less, it is not just talk when I say, that no other girl has more beautiful discipline in the body than you. I've been to, and seen a lot of places, so you can trust my judgment. But, I'll get back to my own prospects: I'm traveling to Vadsbo parish, then I'll go as far down as Grävsnäs, Sollebrunn and Koberg. I make an annual business trip of sorts; buying and inspecting... I can't go into details... of certain estates and property of the 'S---' family, with whom I am distantly, very distantly, related. From that, I derive an income of a few percent, beyond the pleasure of getting to look around a little. I have never done anyone injustice, and I intend to keep it that way all of my days. My wings don't extend further than that. Still, it could happen that after a few years, I could put together enough money to buy a little farm in Timmelhed, off toward Ulricehamn where I know people. Just as well, I would not try to lure you there. You dislike the country, just as much as I don't especially like small towns, apart from traveling through, and gladly leaving them as fast as I can. You, for your part, are glad and eager when we do. So, that is at least one point wherein we meet. There ought to be more if we just look for them. Whether you wear a silk scarf, or a hat, I like you both ways. You write in a good, readable hand. Finally, I have a taste for planting flowers in the spring and summer…"

"In pots?"

"No, dammit, in open ground, or, at least in cold-frames, if the flowers are of a sort that can't tolerate cold soil. But, why not in pots, too, to have in the window?"

"White wallflowers?"

"Absolutely. They do well, and give the room a nice smell. But then one must…"

"Yes, then one must have window panes of pure, completely clear, white glass, Albert! For, the coarse, greenish glass, that some poor citizens have to be pleased with, looks so bad with beautiful flowers, that it's better not to have it in their windows. Otherwise, I like lavender very much. It has grey-blue flowers that go so well in rooms where one lives, if one is less wealthy. Oh Albert! You should see my little room… I have wallflowers! Although it is true, that you are traveling with me only as far as Mariestad, and I shall be traveling alone on that bare, sandy coast between Mariestad and Lidköping. Oh, that is the ugliest, most desolate road! I get anxious when I think of that part of the journey that I must make."

"Why should I break off at Mariestad? It is not decided yet. Instead, why not begin the ugly road, as you call it, on the other side of Mariestad. One has, if nothing else, the wonderful Kinne Hill to travel past between Mariestad and Lidköping"

"Well, it may be that there is Kinne Hill somewhere, but it is flat in those parishes, as I recall. I have traveled to Mariestad from Lidköping. The land is worthless, too, whether it's flat or not. But I shiver at the thought that…"

"What, is she in a state for trembling?" thought Albert. "Well praise God! Then she is still…" "Why are you trembling, Sara?" he said aloud.

70

"Well, I can tell you, although it sounds a little childish. I think it's tedious to ride a farm wagon next to a pile of stuff. Therefore, I seldom go out on jobs in the outlying parishes, but mostly send a journeyman, or one of the more reliable boys, even though I have suffered big losses that way, but, I can't do everything."

"How, in God's name have you suffered big losses?"

"There is pretty well nothing in Lidköping, that careless boys have not beaten to pieces as much on the road, before it even has a chance to be installed. But that problem can be absorbed; it doesn't strike to the heart. Now, I'll get to see how my poor mother is doing when I go down there."

"She'll die soon, perhaps, and, as you said, that is probably just as well. Then you will be alone in the house. But, to return to our journey, what will you give me if I come along, not just to Mariestad, but all the way to Lidköping?"

"Oh!"

The little cry of joy was unavoidable. Still, Sara pulled herself together immediately, looked at her comrade, and said, "You shall have, first and foremost, my part of the expenses…"

"Of course."

"And… if you are not opposed, you shall have a wallflower sprig in a new frame, that I shall cut the glass for, underlain with gold paper, and with the sides glued together."

"I am still not completely satisfied. Well, we'll think of something else along the way. We still have many miles ahead of us, before we get there," he said.

"And maybe," she broke in with, her own pretty accent, "You'll become seriously angry with me before we get so far as Mariestad, and we will separate by the time we get there."

The two neat, well crooked, dark mustachios raised up on the sergeant's upper lip, and it is highly probable that he intended to raise the lip itself to open his mouth and speak. Perhaps, it was to more minutely describe his compensation for the toil of traveling to Lidköping. But Sara had hardly finished speaking, when the horses shied at God-knows-what movement by the side

71

of the road. The brown, wrinkled old driver, in his way just as conversational with the horses as the two travelers were with each other, had slackened the reins to slow down, so that he could not quickly draw them up again, and the coursers broke into a gallop, and began to bolt. The horses of Närke are a splendid breed, and are bred well. They are remarkable for their fire, courage, and eagerness to run. Albert himself, therefore, had to rise up and stand in the seat. He jerked the reins from the hands of the old man, and drew them in so hard that both red-black roans had to crook their necks like bows, snorting, and setting their noses against their chests. Thus the run-away was halted, but, as it was, the wheel hubs could have caught fire if they wanted to.

The sergeant's hair flew around the edges of his shako. He felt like he was twenty years younger, again. He looked down to the side. Sara did not look at all anxious during the wild ride, and that pleased Albert more than this writer is able to describe. Albert thought, "Here is yet another point where we meet. Perhaps it will happen again."

But really, it is not impossible for this writer to follow all of the events, and should he not go on telling of everything, large and small, both what was said, and what was not said? What happened, and what did not happen? How often the hat was exchange for the scarf, and vice versa? In short, they went on to Glanshammar, to Örebro, to Kumla, and beyond.

Although their wagon and horses almost ran out of control on the Glanshammar Road, the rest of the journey did not go so quickly as had been estimated at first. Would it be too much to make four overnight stays between Arboga and Mariestad? If they did, then it must be concluded that they would drive into Mariestad on Tuesday. They had, indeed, left Stockholm on Thursday, as already stated, therefore six days in all, of which one was on Lake Mälaren, and the additional five on land.

They were delayed a bit, when they stayed over at Bodarne. When they arose the next morning, Sara was not completely well. She hadn't been subjected to so much movement before,

72

and although her eyes shone brighter than ever, gleaming and full of emotion when she looked at Albert, still, they showed that she had not slept half the night. Thus, the girl who brought coffee at six-thirty was very welcome. "An excellent drink for such an occasion as morning! Or is that too personal to mention?"

"Therefore it is best to be in Mariestad right away. No one can help that the trip has already taken six days."

Mariestad enjoys the well deserved reputation of being one of Sweden's most beautifully situated towns. Who does not remember the open, wide-stretched vista over Vänern, especially from the churchyard? The big, high-placed church itself, which commands the eye's notice, and draws it away to the right (counting from the Stockholm side), from the leafy avenue on which one is traveling. Finally, when you come into the city, and as far down as to the other side of the square, you can see the long floating bridge swimming idyllically on the Tida River's broad, clear water. And now on the other side of the bridge, is the beautiful Marieholm, the governor's mansion, not just dazzling with its unusual height, but is all the more captivating seen through the surrounding trees. Fond memories of the excellent helmsmen of the county seem intertwined between the maple, birch, and hazel branches swaying with their fluttering leaves in the soft afternoon wind.

Who does not remember all that? Still, the memories do depend on one having been there in Mariestad, for merely hearing about them isn't worth much. You must have watched the Tida's inviting, gentle flow with your own eyes.

Albert and his traveling companion arrived there one heavenly beautiful July afternoon. This story-teller must be permitted a little digression here. I believe it forgivable to relate what follows.

After entering the city, and reaching the square, they did not drive straight down to the Marieholm Bridge, but turned down a little street to the right, that did not end until it stopped at Lake

Vänern itself. About in the middle of that street, lay the house that received weary travelers.

They got out here, ensured that their things were carried in, and everything went well. Afterwards, Albert proposed that since it was still so light outside, and lovely, that they take a walk through the city.

Recently, since Bodarne, Sara had become quieter, not just formal... that's not the right word... loftier, and she did not talk about guild-business so often. Beyond that change, one could notice no less than that her usually steely look had changed to a sort of heavenly benevolence and approachability for almost anything Albert wanted.

Without a word of opposition, she let him take her elbow, and followed where ever he wanted to take her. He had no plan for the walk.

It fell most naturally, and of itself, to walk across the square, and down to the floating bridge, stop in the middle, and admire the Tida.

Standing here, and looking northward they had an unlimited view over Lake Vänern's watery expanse in the clear afternoon sunlight. They could not see where, or how, the lake flowed seamlessly into the firmament itself. It seemed to be all one. "And this is called the Tida?" she asked, with a little shake of her head. The Lida flows through our city just like this, and one has just as great... great... great view over Vänern, and upward right up to the sky, when it is evening like it is now. Oh Albert! I am reminded of the time when my mother and I stood on the bridge above the Lida... and she threw... threw the ring away... far... far out..."

Albert flinched, and took her under the arm and went, despite her reluctance, back off of the Tida Bridge. Arriving back up in the city again, they turned toward the area where the church stood. The cemetery, surrounded by a low stone wall, and planted in trees in several groups, lies so near Lake Vänern that one seems to have the lake right below. And one seems to have the tall, grey, awe-inspiring church, right beside.

Sara asked to sit on a gravestone. Albert sat beside her. "You are so silent, good, beloved Sara. Are you tired?" She answered not even once to his words, but he followed her gaze. He noticed that she was watching a pair of beautiful children playing in the grass, a little distance away, long, and almost dreamily, (as he had never seen her before). They were running, and chasing, and swatting each other's faces with wallflowers.

The children looked neither poor nor rich, but they did look especially pretty. Albert waved them over, to please Sara. They came, bare-headed and long haired. With difficulty, Sara held back a glimmering tear, said nothing, but caressed them around their necks and faces.

Albert said, "Just think, Sara, if these children had no parents."

"They cannot be without father and mother, because they exist."

"But, if their father and mother were…"

"Dead? Yes, but still protected by God, and by good people. There's always someone. I know a couple in Lidköping who have no children, but take pleasure in providing clothes and help for small children, out of their own pocket, whose parents… Albert…"

"Dead?"

"No, much worse! They abused and dissipated each other, in body and soul, and included the children."

"You, yourself were one of those beaten children at one time, Sara?"

"That I am as human as I am, I can thank a kind-hearted aunt, Aunt Gustava, who used to sneak over to my parent's house. When Papa died, it got much calmer, and better at home. But Mama was already so destroyed, and withdrawn, that she couldn't do anything, and could no longer bring herself back, although otherwise, there would have been a possibility for her to become human again. Since then, I have grown up, and taken up the reins at home. But I am such that, I can testify of myself, I never want to harm, or humiliate anyone, least of all you. It is terrible, and always will be, that a person should get an entitlement, whereby she is put in a position of devastating someone else when she dies. God's beautiful love doesn't gain any progress in the world that way. I never want power over another, and I don't think I want to give it to anyone else over me."

Silent, Albert patted the child on the head.

"Oh, you like little children," she cried.

Without answering, he said, "Now, if these children's parents were unmarr…"

"The children look beautiful and good, as God and humans love them."

"But if the parents are not marri… don't look after them… instead of these children, we could be seeing starving, ragged, abandoned waifs."

"If the parents are wise and good," she interjected mildly, "they will watch after their children, so long as they live, that I know, as surely as that no one tears his own heart out."

"But if the parents are cruel, and lack good sense?"

"In that case they are bad and stupid, whether they are married or not. Therefore, they act, against the children, against themselves, and against God's creation. I have seen, and observed that enough, Albert."

"But there is a difference…"

"Yes, a big difference. You see, the difference I have seen is; if people begin by being good and wise, they can go that way, and even grow up like that, if they are allowed to live their own lives as God created them. Or they can meekly be controlled by people, whereby they go wrong, as often happens. But, if they are brought up to spend night and day at odds with each other, they are stricken in body and soul. And if they despise that company, but are forced to remain together, as so often happens, they grow embittered and angry, and become like devils."

Albert winced, as always, at the word 'devil'; a swear-word he, himself, never used as an epithet. He whispered something to himself about 'Readers'.

"Think what you want, Albert, but I am certainly not a 'Reader'. You can ask them, for I leave you in full freedom to do so.

When I speak of devils, on this gravestone here, I mean horrible, ruined people that one can observe in the cities, and in the country, too, I believe."

"In that way, people are tested, Sara."

"Tested? I think that no one who wishes people well, places such a test, where the greatest number of them fail. And who is it, who, properly and respectably, places people in such a test from hell, that it ends in hell itself? I don't call that a test. I call it madness."

Albert flinched again, and leapt up at these perilous words. 'Hell, madness and devils were words that had never been used in conversation with acquaintances, except, as previously mentioned, when he swore. He had never uttered a single oath, at least none directed at her, good or evil.

To lift his mood, he lifted up the children, one after the other, in his arms, and kissed them warmly and looked a little shyly down at her on the gravestone. He found her, at that moment, looking up at him and the children, and it seemed as if she half-intended to stretch her arms out for them. He was captivated by the tableau. He was not a painter, composer, nor poet. Therefore, he could not draw, sing, nor tell what he felt looking at the seated woman looking up at him. She was not poetic either. Still, that image of pure, guileless heavenliness was something.

"Now, now let's go in, Sara! The evening is falling. You'll get cold. I wouldn't want you to catch cold for a thousand worlds. He gave the children several kisses more, and a few small silver coins. They ran along their way, singing. He took her under the arm.

"Catch cold? I hope that doesn't happen. I am quite warm, although you should never see me heated, or see my cheeks glow."

Before they walked out of the cemetery, she turned around and looked at the tall, majestic, grey church steeples behind them, and made an imperceptible bow, as if curtsying farewell from there. Or, perhaps it was in thankfulness for the pleasure that she had enjoyed with the children in the graveyard.

Albert's heart grew light again, when they came back out onto the street. She, too, walked lightly, carefree, and almost lithely by his side. They began to talk about the trip, and all the necessities for it. Before they knew it, they had come to the inn, where their belongings had already arrived in a beautiful, spacious, cheerful room.

So, it soon got so dark, that a maid came with candles, rolled down the curtains and asked what would the gentle-folk order this evening? And would they like to eat in the dining room, or alone in their room?

"Let's begin by getting a menu, little Miss, and then we'll decide on the rest."

The girl left. "Would you enjoy being among the people down there?" asked Albert.

"Not... and especially not in the evening!" she said. "We are now in Mariestad, and we have a little to discuss and work out with each other, in case we separate here, and you go south, and I go west. Let's eat up here."

The girl returned with the menu. Albert chose his dishes, which agreed with Sara's, except that she had a salad with her cutlet, and he, on the other hand, had his favorite; cucumbers. "Set the table for us up here," he said. The maid left, and came back and everything was put in good order. After the end of the happy, enchanting little meal-time, the table was cleared again, and they were alone.

## Chapter Seven

*"But that's what I was saying: that if you travel around a little, I have nothing against that. And I want to set myself up at home, completely alone. Forget? If you jumped up right now, and traveled to Solle springs tonight, would you forget me for it?"*

When they were alone, as mentioned at the end of the previous chapter, Sara went over to their luggage, and began to separate the things that belonged to Albert. Are you leaving immediately tonight, or first thing in the morning?" she asked, as if with half a voice.

"Where do you mean?"

"I don't know where you are going, Albert. But you spoke of turning south at Mariestad to the big estates?"

"We've already passed through, and left Vadsbo parish, where I have some things to see to. I'll get to them on the way back. For sure, I am going to Odensåker, Skövde, and yes, all the way down to Marka and Grolanda, so the best way would be from here out to Lexberg, turn off at Kekestad, and not follow the west road through Björsäter, and on to Lidköping. But I also have business in Grävsnäs, to Sollensbrunns area, and the road there goes quite comfortably through Lidköping. Why could I not just as well go the reverse way right now?"

"Why do you say? You have the freedom to go whichever way you want."

"Yes, Sara, for my own business, I certainly have the freedom…"

"Is there something else to prevent you? Which do you yourself want?"

"You ask me, Sara, when you know as well as I do, that I want to go along with you to Lidköping. May I not see your little house? May I not see the little rooms one-floor-up that can be rented to, for instance, to travelers? And the bigger room on the ground floor, where you think someday to have a boutique, which could happen soon enough, if your mother…"

79

"You really want to see all that?"

"Good, beloved Sara... you're smiling? I'm absolutely serious. I have a lot of travel to do here in West Gothland, there and back, in the summer, and maybe all year, if my plan to get a transfer to the West Gothdal Regiment, which depends on Dorchimont. Somewhere along the routes, I must have a home, for the sake of my stuff... Couldn't I rent those little rooms one floor up from you?"

"In Lidköping? But you haven't seen the rooms yet. Save it until then. Never rent or buy what you haven't seen and inspected!"

That golden rule struck a chord, and it was the first of sort that the sergeant heard from Sara's lips. But the words fell so nicely, and were conveyed in an almost caressing tone. They stood at one of the room's windows. They had not rolled down the curtains, and had snuffed the candles in order to enjoy the captivating view for a while, before they went to bed.

"In your Lidköping suite, Sara, there is surely rosy wallpaper. That never fails. And inside, surely, at some time in the past, you've had occasion to grind chalk?" He held her in his arms. She looked questioningly up into his face, to see if he were making fun of the dream she had told him; the dream in Arboga. But now, she found no irony; no satire on his lips. "In the past?" she interjected. "That could happen many times yet... I don't intend to abandon my work."

"But if I rent the suite?"

"Then I'll keep my things in my place, on the bottom floor."

"Do you not want to work upstairs with me?"

If you are going to live there, there is a lot that you'll have to take care of on your own, and have in order, as you might require. There's a good restaurant in the neighborhood and cheap cleaning service is easy to get. There's even washing and ironing by accommodating folk, who only get a little bit for compensation, Albert. They could make more, if not for the guilds. But I do say that I will often wish that I may invite you down for a little, simple brunch, if it is convenient. And perhaps you will invite me up, too. But I want never, never to take what is yours, or involve myself in your household business. I will just answer if you ask my advice, that you can then follow or not, as you want. Most of all, I don't want to hinder your work. I don't understand your business; it must be a lot of writing, and accounting, maybe, as you do inspect... yes, just as well... Horstadius and Selander and Silfver... maybe at Koberg... but I never want to disturb you in it."

"I thank you for that, Sara, that's outrageously great. But isn't there anything that can be in common with two such people who...?"

"There's really a lot; yet very much more to have in common, besides those things, Albert. Can I tell you straight out what I mean? I've thought about it these last few days..."

"And I've thought about it, too. A lot, you can believe. It must become our top priority."

"Still, we should be careful that it doesn't fall apart for us, by being too eager. To take things easy and smart is to have it half-won, you know. Pure and simple, Albert. That is how to take things, when two people love each other."

The sergeant didn't completely understand her, but he caressed her beautiful hair at her forehead. "Go on, dear Sara. You talk first."


"She lifted her head from his chest, where she had been resting it, thought for a moment, and said, "Because it is so, that you love me, and I love you, we have that in common. That is a lot, Albert. And that is more than many have. But if we undertake to have a lot of inconsequentials in common, I can tell you what will follow. If you take my little house, my business, my furniture, and money... not much, but what I have, and can get... yes, I can't deny that I could start to grow shrewish. Maybe you don't know how to take care of such things. I'm guessing that you don't know that yourself yet, as you have not had a house, and a trade, at least, so far as I know. And It's very possible that my concerns are not justified, and that you can handle everything

81

very well. However, should that concern, Albert... yes, I can tell you, that as soon as you saw such behavior from me, you will get angry. Then I'd go off by myself, and chew on my secret thoughts. For a while, I'd think I had done you an injustice. Then I'd think I could just as well be right, at least in part. The time wasted on all these battles, and torments of the mind and soul, could be used for something useful and profitable. And if time is wasted, that is still the least of it. Albert, I would become so grouchy. You would find me irritable, first sometimes, then more often. That would make you testy, too. Or, if we both repressed the unpleasantness, kept it in, and swallowed it, as they say, the resentment would creep into the marrow of our bones, wear away our health, and we would wither in body and soul. Then we would surely start taking the waters at Lundsbrunn, or perhaps squander money on the mud I've heard talk about in Porla, or Locka: such things that hardly do any good when one is in a bad way. So, another thing, too, Albert, that I want you to mark well. From suffering, my skin would soon go bad, my eyes would pale, and I would grow uglier than I am now. You wouldn't have the heart to tell me so, but you would think it often. I would probably figure it out myself and go off alone in my dark brooding over what you think of me, and what you never told me; I would certainly figure it out on my own. Then I would start sleeping badly, and that will make me more wrinkled day by day. Yes, Albert, there is no limit to the ugliness, when one starts to go that way. I've seen that in people. And how would it go for you? If you were the best one could find, you would try to comfort me with mild words, but however well you meant, it would sound empty in my ears because I would see that you lied to appease me. That would just make things worse, rather than better. In any case, you would probably also grow melancholy, for you are human, Albert, just like me. Still, you would not get as tired of my losing my looks, as for my inner irritability, tediousness, and the whole ugliness of the soul. Perhaps the torment will, in the end, make me unwise and treacherous, then I will become even more insufferable to you. And what one usually says about promises and vows becomes just empty words, where no person still holds what no person can hold. I'm talking about the inner heart's love for another person, which is the only thing of value, but which, without help, goes away if a person, in his spirit, becomes unbearable. I have now told you how I could become insufferable to you. It could also happen, perhaps, that you could become unbearable to me. What comfort is there in the words given? One sits alone and unhappy, but has a name. It is a title without meaning. It's like a sign outside a shop, and when one goes in and asks for merchandise, there are no wares that the sign advertises. What do you do then? You leave angry, and spit at the sign. Isn't that pleasant? Many times, I have been mortified to see that in others, and I don't like it. I don't want it like that for you or me. If you love me to the soul, then I am happy, and that is enough, and I'll take care of myself for the rest of my life, happy, and contented, and diligent. I'll sleep well at night, and be pretty in the daytime. I know this, and you shall get to see it. But if you don't love me, then what good is anything else, and what would I do with everything else? The most legitimate, and best for us is simply that love must be enough. And, maybe it still might end, but at least we can avoid those things that can be predicted to cause humiliation and thwart love and not help it."

 "But Sara, if we are good, wise people, as I think we both are, we should, right from the beginning, be able to… and then still… and I don' think we should count on the unhappy example you gave."

"If we are good, wise people, as I hope, with God's help, we might be… so, Albert, isn't it all the better? We need nothing more, than to practice what goodness and wisdom direct toward each other, and toward all others, wherever we go. Who can prevent that? Think about it now, if we are good and wise, then isn't it all the more important that we continue to love each other? That must be the thing. Then we must particularly avoid such things that can humiliate or make one nasty, phony, and dumb. It is always up to God how a person continues to be, and many can fall. But, at least, we should not stir up those things in which there is a credible likelihood that it can fill the heart with pustulence, and the brain with a foggy sky. Others may call it a test, I call it evil and unwise enterprise, that people do not have the right to do to each other. If God, Himself, gives someone a torment that cannot be avoided, then he must patiently withstand it, and it is a test. But people don't have to create ugly situations; such are avoidable, and ought to be avoided, and not be called 'test', as they most often go to hell, where well no ordinary institution ought to want to draw its subjects. But if you don't think the same as I do, Albert, then you have your full freedom…"

"In any case," broke in the sergeant, "Sara, you have it wrong, that there is misery and unhappiness in every house."

"In every one?" she asked, "I have seen one or two households where they live well, really well. But it's certainly not because they were "read-together", which was of no help, otherwise. It's because they draw agreement in heart and soul, at least as much as needed, which always helps, if it is there."

"'Read-together'? What do you mean by that?"

"That someone read over them. Dear Albert, mumbo-jumbo serves no purpose. One must once go so far into this thing, as in all others, to seek what really serves, and not build on the untenable. From that, the only result is unhappiness, and, what is worse, really bad behavior. For, as soon as two people don't love one another, it's really ugly behavior that…"

"Mumbo-jumbo? But I really like a beautiful prayer… such, for example, that are said when two…"

Sara looked up with a wonderful expression. "God is my witness," She said, barely audibly. "God knows that I love prayers. I say them, and I think I always shall. But, oh, I don't pray for what there is no use for. That is mumbo-jumbo and empty sounds, if not yet worse, namely; blasphemy. Prayers? Oh great God! Not even the most beautiful prayer turns white to black, or black to white. If two stand beside each other, and lie

84

about feelings for each other that they do not have, prayer will not make a lie into truth. And if, they do not lie, but still promise such things that they have no power to keep; is that canceled through some reading over them? And what happens most often, is that later they cannot do what is impossible to do, but still, for appearances, pretend, so that the lies and misery increase. What then, did the poor prayer prevent? It did not keep things from turning out the way they did. And when they stay with each other, they become all the more coarse in soul and body... yes, real depravity, one must admit... in the end they no longer remember what beautiful and clean in the world is, or understand anything fundamentally wise about people, however much they are read-over. You see it all the time, and I call it immorality, Albert, and it is not worthy of being called good, noble, or happy, if it isn't. It's never worth winning, if one uses other than that which one wins with, I think. When I am out of oil for putty, I don't stand there and pray over the putty. I go out and get some oil to mix the putty with, and that is what helps. I never use mumbo-jumbo, Albert, although many in Lidköping throw salt in the oven if they have a toothache, or pour lead over sick people, and stick splinters in trees. Sometimes, they say they get cured, as can happen, but it doesn't happen from splinters, I don't think. So, Albert, one meets those who are 'read-together' who are moral and live well, but that doesn't come, in itself, from the reading."

"Well, at least it doesn't hurt."

"Yes, but. For, once two such people have been 'read-over', who do nothing for each other, than to bring each other humiliation and misery, then it is still wanted, and still maintained that they be together, and tear each other apart, merely for the sake of a reading-over that happened unnecessarily. I mean, that is harmful. It is badly done, to use prayers to no use. In most cases it does really dreadful damage. Oh my God... and to make prayers, which are so holy and lovely when they go to the right place; that is what I know best."

"Beloved girl, when did you pray last?"

"In Arboga... Albert." She whispered it so quietly, and it almost sounded like a 'my' came before the name 'Albert'. But the whole expression was too magical to maintain, although one second of it, was so deeply felt, that eternity would be lost in it. After a silence, she said aloud, "I'll say it one more time, Albert, if you don't think the same as I, then you have full freedom of yourself, and yours. Speak now; for in that case I would rather that you travel tonight, or in the morning, and not come with me to Lidköping, although, God knows how glad I have been to have you with me, on that sandy, awful road."

"Only on the road?"

Their warm gazes met, but they did not look into each other's eyes for long, before they turned to look out the window at the sky, which seemed not to have darkened, but lingered a long time in twilight. Albert sat in a chair by the window with Sara on his knee, and remembered away beyond Bodarne, to that black night in Arboga, when, then too, he sat by the window, and vainly struggled to scratch his name in the glass. How much things had changed since then. What a new era. With what transformed eyes did he look at her. And she, herself, seemed to have entered into another world. All of the previous recurring sharp, witty, impishness was gone. Now she had the look of a fellow citizen, with the same sensibility in all, as before, with a wisdom imbued with the scent of innermost devotion, and purest sweetness. The most wonderful part was the complete freedom in that, if he left and traveled without her, when he wanted, and where he wanted, despite everything about her, it far from tempted him to abandon her, but rather, made her a thousand times more loveable, bright and delightful in his eyes. "And a true heart is the only... only... thing that attracts true love. Perhaps it could be missing, but if anything will work, it is only a true heart," he thought.

"What are you looking at in the heavens, Sara?"

"I wonder, is it far?"

"He pressed her to his chest, and answered, "We are on our way."

"Just on our way?"

"No, we are there… if…"

"Albert!"

"Tell me, Sara, honestly… you were just talking about how people can grow ugly from worry and torment of the soul; and you were certainly right. We'll let that be. But Sara, say… you could never grow ugly. That seems impossible."

"In our souls, Albert, you and I never need grow ugly, and I think that well enough. But you know well that the body, when one grows old, well… even without the toll of misery."

"What do aging looks mean, when a good and true spirit is reflected purely in the eyes and all the constellations of wrinkles' expressions? That is the heaven I am drawn to."

"I think so too. Thank God you are not a fool, Albert."

"And even the body falls apart late, really late, so long as a good, lively, industrious spirit lives in it. That's what I believe, Sara."

"I have seen it in my aunt Gustava," she said.

"Let us have it so, Sara, that each of us takes care of his or her own. I shall not let you have a hand in mine, just as you will not give me control over yours. We shall only have our love in common. But what if either of us fell into need, so that one's own was not sufficient for life and maintenance?"

"Will love not give assistance, then?" she asked, sitting up straight. If you came to need, Albert, would I not give to you of what I have, so long as I have it, and never find you to be a wastrel, a bum. And If I became very poor, so it could even happen that you… you would be willing to give me something?"

"God, you ask, Sara! But when it is like that between us on both sides, don't we already have our means in common?"

"No, the difference is as big as the sky. If I give you a gift of money or something else, then you do with it, and handle it any way you want. That way, no misunderstandings arise. It will be yours, just as if you had had it before. And, if you ask me for advice on how to use it, then I shall answer you, and then you can do with the advice what you think is best. In that way, regardless of the gift, you are just as free, unobligated, and undisturbed. In the same way, if you honor me with something, then you must give it on the same conditions; as a pure and loving gift for enjoyment and use, that I may direct and employ as I please, and need. Such gifts and gifts in return, are then a help to the person, but not a mutual blight, like the daily hassles that people usually make for each other."

"Then people can never keep house together?"

"They can certainly try. If it goes well, then they can keep right on with it, just as one does with a lot of other things that go well. If it goes badly, then it is a good idea to stop it, just as with anything else that goes badly. But love between two people must be kept in peace and calm, and never be made to suffer, or be dependent on cohabitation or housekeeping, however it unfolds. I think it is best that they never move in together, I'll tell you that. That's because people who love each other irritate, anger, and in the end, destroy each other much more quickly than others who don't depend on each other. They see each other a little more cool-headedly. In the end, if they attempt that unnecessary pleasure; to let two heads govern worldly things that are best managed when they are not mixed together, but owned by each person to himself, who acts according to his own mind, they may, at least, be smart enough to call it quits before they fall out of love, which can easily happen. For no glass is more beautiful than the heart's affection, and no enamel more fragile. I understand that."

"That way, it would be best if we not only skip living together, but not see each other too often, either."

"Aren't you thinking of travelling a lot, Albert?" she said with a look that was anything but cruel.

"I must. I can't avoid it."

"How gladly I'll think of you when you are gone. And so beautiful; as then I will have you in my soul, and that would be difficult for you if you stayed home. But then you'll return! And every time you'll be twice as welcome!"

"But, my God!..."

"In that way love will be enough. You shall escape seeing me in all the stupid, tedious, yes…ugly, times when it's best not to see each other. And if you have such times, for you are human, Albert, I won't have to see you then, either."

"But, by the living God, Sara, I don't understand. Where will that go? Can we invent a way to forget each other?"

"Those who wear each other away with repeated insufferability forget each other more quickly, Albert. If they remember each other, it's a painful memory, like an abscess."

"How?"

"It's close bodies with distant souls. Like it says in the scriptures: they praise me with their lips, but their hearts are far away from me."

"You are a Reader after all!"

"I like close souls and distant bodies better, if it's to be that way."

"But, can't both be close?"

"Sometimes, Albert. It's like that with us, right now. But…And I want you to come along to Lidköping. But I will tell you this; if you then go travelling around, I have nothing against it. And I want to run my house completely alone. –Forget? If you jumped up now, and ran off, and travelled to Sollebrun tonight, would that make you forget me?"

"Sara, you shall stand before me always!"

"–And I should see you through all of my windows. Try! Travel for serenity's sake."

"Let me slow down a bit."

"Forget? When indifference comes between people, then it is as if forgetfulness comes limping along, in a relationship. But travel and distance, what do they mean? Highways are not what make distance between souls. Well, I don't want you to be gone for more than a half a year, I'll say that."

"You breathe so pretty!"

"Forget?" she said after a moment's silence. Perhaps, if it happens that love ends between people, that forgetfulness can also come. But at least it is certain, and this I know, the heart's

89

joyful memory of ones who squander love itself never fades. Therefore…"

"Okay, I won't see you, and I won't visit too often, Sara. But if I could rent your suite of rooms to sit and do my own work, then nothing in the world, not even you, Sara, can keep me from painting your picture before me; not with a brush, you see, I can't do that… Oh, if I could! And if you get sick, then I'll go down and sit by your bed."

"Sickness comes, dear Albert. I would rather have Maja with me. She understands better."

"But, my god… if… I was just thinking… if, for example, I, myself, got sick?"

"That is a completely different thing. Then I'll go up to your room, and sit with you by your bed night and day, if necessary. I'll close up the shop, and put up a sign saying 'away traveling'. That's the difference, you know, that if a guy is sick… really, when it isn't just talk and he's seriously sick in bed… it's not really unpleasant, tedious, or ugly to be there with him. I can do it. But an ailing, bed-ridden old woman, with tuberculosis or something is best by herself, Albert. Still, if something happens to me, I have nothing against you sticking around in town… in the house… on the upper floor. If…"

"God, what does your wonderful expression mean?"

"If I should, then, come near death, Albert, I want you to come down to my room just before I die… to me!... and… I want to kiss your hand the last of all in the world."

## Chapter Eight

*Look around and put on a happy face! I want the secret joy, that when you ride down the street, every second girl will stop and think, "Wow, there goes a good looking officer!"*

History and geography, who always lend each other a hand, must help each other here, too. So that when the former drew hastily aside, and turned back, the latter began to talk, and speak in the following way: The road between Mariestad and Lidköping stretches all the way from Mariestad to Lidköping. The two travelers began on that road immediately the next morning, as soon as they had dunked their ruskets in a pair of beautiful, real cups.

The geography of West Gothland may say everything it wants and pleases about the southern shores of Lake Vänern. What is certain is that if one is not watching the road that stretches forth here, what meets the eye is not at all unpleasant. When the two travelers reached Bresäter, Albert said, "Now it's a matter of whether we should, starting at Forshem, take the divine road over Kinnekulle, which runs through the north part of the area, so: Medlplana and Källby and on the way we come past Hönsäter, Hällkis and Råbäck..."

"Råbäck? I have heard of Råbäck! I have never been there before," Sara continued, "But why would I go there now that she doesn't live there anymore."

"Who is she?"

"An angel lived there, but has moved to Vättern."

"Mrs... I know... I don't remember the name correctly. I haven't seen her, either," Sara went on. "But if she still lived in Råbäck, then I'd want to take that road. She has lent good, excellent books to Aunt Gustava I Lidköping, and we have read them together between times."

"I want to read them, too!" cried the sergeant. "You shall so... but..."

"Yes. We can choose the other way," he continued. "Go down to Enbacken, east and south of Kullen, through Skälvum, past Husby, and so on. Which shall we take?"

"How can I decide? I don't understand all this."

"You should know, Sara, that Hällkis is among the most remarkable places in West Gothland. It deserves for us to go that way."

"If you want to. And if there are large houses and buildings, then it is worth getting to know the place. There could be some money in it someday."

A little subdued, the sergeant reefed his poetic sails. He had not heard mention of business priorities in a few days, but noticed immediately that they were close at hand. And why should he be bothered at her for it? Just the same, he did not want such heavenly places as Hönsäter, Hällekis, and Råbäck to be sacrificed on the altar of the glassmaster's desires. So, he decided to take the prosaic stretch over Enebacken, and left Kullen to the right-hand side. "On the other hand, she has been high-minded," the sergeant continued, to himself. "Yes, for a couple of days! And her conversational topics, always consistently intelligent, on the other hand, didn't always have the taste of a journeyman in women's clothes. That poor, good, innocent girl!" he said, with a barely restrained tear. "Good, beloved! How unfairly I judged you. Isn't really good that you are so sensible? You shall honestly and excellently take care of yourself and those you…"

He jerked at the horses, as if a sudden fright had come, and he was afraid that they would run off somewhere. He collected himself, and continued on inwardly: "I shall give them all that I can save and put aside, and it shall be a completely pure gift, as she would have it, without any involvement on my side (and without free advice), to keep house with. But? Good God! I shall call them mine! That shall, that must, be my decision!"

"That you shall, and it is my heavenly joy to hear you say so." Stunned, Albert drove to the side of the road at Sara's slowly spoken words. Had he forgotten himself in his dreamy reverie to

92

the point of speaking aloud, and betraying his inner-most thoughts?

"Don't be afraid, Albert. I can hear your whispers; your quietest whispers to yourself; for I am someone who can hear."

"Great God! Who are you? Have you greater abilities than others?"

"You drive so superbly, Albert. I love you. You love me, but you don't answer me."

"How shall I answer? How could you hear what only my trembling soul was thinking?"

"I love your soul. Therefore I hear what your soul's words."

"What?"

"What you want to say; I understand. I perceive your thoughts; even what you were pondering just a bit ago…"

"What, about work?"

"Yes, yes… Albert… a window pane is not so trifling as you think, Albert. It protects you against cold in the winter, and still gives you light. Most things in life aren't like that. So that if it gets warmer it does not happen without darkness, or if there is light it seldom happens without cold. A window alone…mark well, Albert… gives light without letting the cold stream in, and it holds the heat in and preserves the light both. That is the constitution of a window, and it means more than many realize. Therefore, you shouldn't disdain windows, and you shouldn't disdain Sara's trade whereby she has fed herself and everyone in Lidköping that needed her help, and shall continue to do so, including you, Albert, if you come to need."

"No, Sara, you'll never need to do that. Industry! A great diligence in my work… for I too have a trade… good, beloved girl, I feel like heaven to be so industrious. I wish to, and shall, deserve! That word that used to sound so meaningless in my ears. I want to deserve! Work, and thereby, help not just myself, but everyone in Lidköping who needs it from me. Trade and industry… you, Sara, have taught me the right words! He took her hand.

Geography is a poor fellow, who constantly lets himself be overrun by history. Where was it now, when the latter took over? Yes, on the way to Enebacken. So let's go there and stick with geography!

Enebacken... and then you get Holmestads, Göteneds, Skalvum's churches, including Vettlösa, a little distance to the right: pardon me, it's Vättlösa, [Vettlösa means 'witless']. Later, one comes to where one can see Husby and even Kleva Church up on the next hill. Further, the eye soon falls upon Broby Church, Källby Church, Skeby Church... so many churches was inconceivable.

But now the churches are done. A great expanse of water approaches from the right, and strikes the travelers gaze with a thousand hazards; he fears that he will have the entire lake Vänern over him, at least up to the wheel hubs, and there is no doubt that the low, golden beach he was driving on had once lain under the billowing waves. Vänern is fey, and has drawn away a little. Who knows if she won't one day come to herself and suddenly, spontaneously, resume her old domains? It's particularly frightful when the storms come from the north.

Today, the wind fell mute and the waves smiled. Sara sat in expectation of seeing Lidköping at any moment. She felt delight inside.

There is one thing, however, that this narrative must mention: The rare pleasure they enjoyed the whole way, of getting a buggy. Otherwise, wagons are usually a hazard to travelers who don't bring their own wheels, or if they stand in the bottom of the cart, itself. Wagons can be awful to ride on. So, they had themselves a comfortable ride, here. Perhaps the explanation lies nearest to, what the Medicis, who otherwise never meddled with fate, said about Nature; namely, that She has a distinct and particular care for the Woman; that She is reluctant to harm her; that She is reverent, deferential, respectful. That is a mystic, but a holy thought. Therefore the man must step just as reverently aside. We must bend our knees for a heaven that unknown...

94

misunderstood… that stands around us, so near, so good, so secretive, so hidden, and yet so constant.

For the sergeant, the joy of traveling by buggy was such, that when he saw that the horses were good, he would skip hiring a driver, and drive them himself, which the farmers, seeing that they were running properly, agreed to thankfully. In that way, the sergeant and she now traveled alone the entire time.

Lidköping came. They began to ride in the city's first street; broad, big, and good, but a little unevenly stone-paved. "Dear Albert, let me get off here. This is my home-town. I want to go on foot from here. You can drive, I'll go on alone."

"No. I'll get out too, and walk along beside and drive."

"Not! That would look bad. And besides, Albert, there is one other thing. Go by yourself to the inn on the other side of the square. I will go to my house. I want to go there alone first. I want to see how things are with my poor mother."

"I want to see her too."

"No, Albert. If she is still alive, she would feel dread at your appearance. I don't want that."

"My god, what are you saying?"

"You could not possibly avoid betraying yourself. You would behave toward me in such a way that she would see you as a suitor. She would shiver at the prospect of seeing you as her daughter's husband-to-be. I would have a hard time convincing her that never in the world will you be…"

"Ha!"

"Never fear, though, dear Albert. You shall soon come to our home, and get to inspect the rooms you intend to rent. But wait until I call for you. Now, drive straight ahead. It's not hard to find your way, here in Lidköping. Don't turn and you will come as far as that bridge we talked about, over the Lida… that one."

"Ha!"

"Drive over the bridge, but observe the view to the right and left, for no other river as beautiful as the Lida runs through any city. A little further along the same way, you'll come to the square. There is no larger square in the world. Drive straight

95

ahead over it to the street furthest away to the left. That street leads to another tollhouse, from which the road runs to Gothenburg. When you come to that street, just the next cross street from the square, the inn is there on the corner. Go in there, and have all of our things carried up there. Get a room for the night or until I call for you. I'll send an apprentice from home for my things. Can you tell them apart?"

"It doesn't say 'S.V.' on all of them, but I'll try."

"You are absent-minded, dear Albert. When you get there, eat a little something. Strengthen yourself. And don't think about me so much. At least you recognize your own stuff? Everything that isn't yours is mine, so let the boy fetch it."

"What isn't yours is mine!"

"Don't be like that! You're in a decent town, I'll have you know. Look at the people when you drive down the street. You'll see that almost all the girls are lovely… Lidköping is famous for that… I am among the least of them. Look around, and enjoy the view. I want the secret joy of knowing that when you drive down the street, every second girl will stop and think, 'Wow, there goes a fine looking officer!'"

The sergeant nodded a cheerful adieu to Sara as she alit from the buggy. He drove on, still slowly, and often looked over at his travelling companion.

"You're driving too slowly," she said, waving. "That's not suitable for a man." He cracked the whip in the air and the horses took off. Sara Videbeck walked alone.

She turned down to a street along the river. The street led to her home. It was not late in the evening, but it was already afternoon. Several clouds in extended, raggedy, and unexplainable shapes drew here and there over the firmament; still, it didn't look like rain. Descending in the west, the Sun jested with the serious, thoughtful, thin, grey cloud-figures.

The lady walking down the street stopped at a cross street, as people were coming, and she sought a familiar face among them. In small towns almost everyone knows each other. Sara could tell who they were, but locked in deep conversation and some

96

distance away, she could not tell much. She wondered at their behavior; pointing and head-turning. When they had passed, she too walked on, and approached the next corner. Again she stopped short, for a procession was coming. Reverence for such things had always held her back, all the more now, when she was surprised and shocked to see her own journeymen in the procession, dressed in black. Some of the older apprentices, and other acquaintances, were carrying a coffin. It was her mother's! There could be no doubt.

The heaving of her breast, her labored breathing, told her to calm down, for an unsuitable appearance must be avoided. She didn't wish to show herself in travelling clothes, instead of all in black. "My mother, my mother! May I never see your face again?" she cried, wringing her hands, and drawing yet closer onto the corner where she stood, to let the sad procession pass by. She thought she heard the parish clerk softly mumble to his neighbor in the procession, "She died Sunday night."

She paid no attention to the somber wanderers, but when the casket came to the silently weeping daughter, it became impossible for her to continue to her home. She saw that the procession was turning toward the church. She couldn't know if it was to be an interment, or just a viewing. However she was drawn irresistibly to follow along at a distance. For her, everything was still a confusing, terrible, all-too-sudden surprise. To see her mother, at least touch her casket with her lips before she was lowered into the ground, was an absolute necessity.

"Died Sunday night?" She spelled out in her thoughts. Where was I then? I left Stockholm on Thursday. If the journey had not drawn out... had not... we could have... I could have been home by Sunday afternoon. Now it is Wednesday! Where were we Sunday night? Where? At Bodarne, she answered herself.

Lidköping's church is differently situated from Mariestad's church, in that, where the latter stands particularly tall, commanding the entire city, and visible everywhere, Lidköping's, on the other hand, is in a corner of town, just so that it can be seen from a distance, for she too is a substantial building... but not so that it immediately lays claim to the eye. She does not have her place by Lake Vänern itself, like Mariestad's church, but is surrounded by one of the more verdant, darker, more enclosed cemeteries.

Sara wanted all the less to approach the procession, as women never go along in such, and those who are grieving, in particular, don't show themselves, least of all at the cemetery at the decisive moment. But Sara had to go to the cemetery! If the intent was to lower the beloved's remains into the earth, then her sight, as sharp as possible, follow the journey to its last perceptible instant.

She found that the town's most inept preacher had been called, and entrusted with carrying out the services. The casket went surrounded by the people who had been the workers at the glassmaster's widow's shop. They were unaccustomed to wearing black, and were now seen badly furnished to a great extent, with borrowed, or at least, out-grown clothes. As Sara watched them pass by, all of their faces looked pale and haggard. Has it been so bad for them in the three weeks I've been gone from home? "No, it must show sorrow and devotion," she hoped. The casket was already well within the cemetery before the daughter, with staggering steps, even dared to go in.

Once inside, she looked around. There were no groups of people around that she could blend into, and that way dare to come nearer to the pile of earth upon which her staring eyes rested. She drew aside to a tall gravestone under a tree. Hiding herself behind it, she could still see her mother's last... final... honors. The church's smallest bell began ringing softly, the minister opened his missal, the clerk took up his psalm book.

At these sounds, Sara sank to her knees in the grass by the gravestone. Tears came welling, and her trembling head sank down against the flower hedge, and her hands caught her falling forehead. "My mother! My mother!" she cried aloud, for she knew that no mortal heard her here. At that, a spiritual feeling filled her heart. "I have fulfilled your wish, Mother! I have obeyed your constant admonition to me. Oh, wherever you are, give me your blessing!"

If the departed's soul could now look around upon what had gone on here, it could have watched the black-clad ones over by the grave itself, who, with care and respect, (although without many words, for the glassmaster's widow's life was not much to praise), busied themselves with the remains. But here under the tree was a beautiful tableau of the future, and the afterworld, kneeling in the joy of heaven and of life. Even more, the spirit could watch with endless bliss. Heavenly virtue, pure morality, and true sense of duty are often unknown, unappreciated, or not seen. The daughter stood hidden, silent in her prayer; no one saw her. A cooling breeze wafted over the flowers.

The psalm verses were short, the bell ringing soon ended, and the minister's words were no more than what was in the missal. Everything ran its course to completion as it should. Nothing was left out, but nothing was added. Under the journeymen's sunken eyes could be seen little bluish patches, highest up on their cheeks. The fresh-faced apprentices took hold of the waiting shovels, and began throwing the earth into the grave.

Albert had reached his decision on the street corner, and had taken a room one flight up at the town inn. Now he was pacing in it, still troubled, curious and waiting for word; at once dejected, delighted and depressed. He looked at the clock; it was seven p.m. It seemed impossible, now, for him to order horses for the journey to Sollebrun first thing tomorrow. However, at eight o'clock he found it to be quite possible. Still, he had to say goodbye to... and when should he return? It wouldn't need a discussion of the most complicated sort. Still, he had already grown accustomed to discussing so much with someone, and he wanted to do so even now, but he found himself alone.

His worry collected now into a single focal point. He sat silent, and stiff, and staring in his corner sofa, wondering why no word came. He heard the hotel maid knock on some of the doors of the rooms outside. He called to her with a thundering voice.

She arrived flying. "Bring me a cup of tea!" he said with a wild look in his eye.

Accustomed to unusual strangers, she meekly went her way silently. Then he called her back, and she returned. "Did you hear what I wanted?" he roared. "Yes sir." "Then make it quick while I'm sitting here waiting!" "The gentleman has not waited for me so much, I don't think," she said offended, and left in a huff.

"Oh, how I am waiting for you!" he burst out with a sigh, without having heard the departing girl.

The tea came, hot and strong. She who carried it looked angry, for anyone can lose patience. When the sergeant brought the cup to his lips he scalded himself terribly and he yelled, "Damn it! Couldn't you have waited with it a little? I was not made to be scalded."

"Neither was I," answered the Lidköping girl combatively. "Are you enraged?"

"No, there doesn't need to be more than one like that. I need to add a little more sugar and cream and it'll cool off," remarked the sergeant, returning to his senses and better mood. "What time is it?"

"That doesn't even matter to me."

"Damn! Aren't you something!"

"Would you like another cup?"

"I see that it is almost nine o'clock and still no word! Make my bed up ASAP. I want to lie down, so I have something to do. Yes, pour another cup!"

"Are you going to drink it in bed?"

"Pour it and let it sit there, I suppose. I'm going out to the street to look around, but if any messages come, call for me immediately. And make the bed in the meantime."

"A strange off'cer," said the girl, after he left. "But, he's waiting for a message, and I don't care anything about him." She threw the bed quickly and hastily together. She was mad. Pillows and sheets ran like a pack of dogs under her hands. ASAP... like he wanted... the bed was ready.

Really melancholy and pale, his head sank to his chest, the sergeant returned. "Has there been no word?" he asked the maid in the meekest voice, as she bounced down the stairs. "No, but everything is in order up in your room." She disappeared into the nether regions. He went up the stairs.

Arriving, he said nothing. He cast another look out the window at the street; to know if… but nothing was to be seen.

He sat a long time by the window, but nothing happened, other than it grew all the greyer around him. "I'm going to bed!" he said finally, aloud, but slowly, as if in a lethargy. There was no word of opposition to his statement. No one was present to oppose him, in the very least.

He undressed lethargically, lay down, and went to sleep, wrapped in the innkeeper's sheet and grey-speckled silk cover; expensive in itself, but worthless to the sergeant.

The next morning… which was a Thursday again, to judge from the evening before, which had been a Wednesday night… the next day it happened that the sergeant awoke. No one said "Good morning," no one arose by his side, no one nodded to him. No one even came in, for, in his distress, he had not ordered breakfast the evening before. However, he was a man, so he got out of bed, and stood up.

"Incomprehensible!" he thought.

He washed his face in cold water, and dressed himself as elegantly as the cut of his uniform allowed, and stepped in front of a big wall mirror to make the final adjustments. The pale, chiseled cheeks, the big dark, love-sick eyes, the great-looking head of hair: the whole image in the mirror looked, in truth, like he had advanced to Crown Prince. With that, anger grew within him, because, for some time now, he had had a decided, and profound desire to remain at the under-officer rank. "Straighten up, you weakling!" he mumbled to himself. Dark flashes arose in the corners of his eyes, and he cast angry, defiant looks at his counter-part in the mirror, who, for understandable reasons immediately returned them. Thus, the two gentlemen braced each other up, and for a while, the sergeant looked like a Swedish Achilles.

Some pattering steps, the door opened, and the maid stepped in with the report that messages had been received last night, and that those rooms to be rented...

"Message? And I did not hear about before now!" Lightning threatened in these words. The girl turned hastily to the door, but caught herself, and explained that the message came so late, that the gentleman had been long asleep, and she certainly did not dare...

"Where did the message come from?"

"From the Videbeck woman."

"The Vide... (again, a lightning-flash, but he could not deny that that could be just the right term for that 'middle-person', over whom he had brooded so much. Still, he could not bring himself to refer to her that way).

"Yes, or from that house, more rightly said," continued the girl, "for the Videbeck woman is finally gone. But the apprentice didn't really know what was going on, and took it to his departed mistresses house."

"Dead? What are you saying! Heavens and Hell! Dead? No... and I wasn't told yesterday?"

The girl answered, surprised, "The message said that this room that was for rent should be visited at eight o'clock in the morning. Therefore, I didn't think it was worth bothering you before seven o'clock."

"The message said 'Arrive at eight o'clock'? Look here, it's a quarter after eight. But... Eternal God! Dead? It's impossible! Impossible! Impossible! Impossible!"

He burst out, and asked at the door for the way to the Videbeck house. The maid told him, and drew it out, as well, as his impatience and her agitation allowed. He hurried off.

The day was wonderfully pretty. The sergeant came down to one of the streets by the Lida. The day's freshness, the new sun, and the blue, the white in the sky, on the trees, on... Oh, the sergeant was probably not in a mood to notice and enjoy it all so much. He should have understood from the story of the last several days, that it was 'the Videbeck woman' the mother, and not at all 'the Videbeck woman' the daughter, who had died. But he was too preoccupied to think about it.

Finally, he saw a little, red, wooden house with a Strängnäs look to it, but well kept up. A long walk strewn with fir twigs met him on the street. His heart was clattering: he was walking the path of the dead.

He walked through a wooden gate with a proper door handle, into a spacious, newly-swept yard. He stepped up onto a low, broad porch step. The door, itself, was fairly large, embellished with maple and birch decorations. The scent of chervil, and elk-grass arose from the floor. When he met the light fragrance, his knees trembled, for he knew that its intent was to conceal the dead-stench.

An elderly woman came to greet him. Nicely, but absolutely simply dressed, with a mixture of worry and goodness on her face. Again, it tore at his heart. "This must be old Maja!" he thought. What could he say? How could he begin? Finally, he stammered, "I have heard that there was a room for rent…"

"To rent! Yes, one floor up, if I may show it to the gentleman."

He went up the stairs, but he was trembling, for what if she were really dead? What in God's name would he do with the room? His foot caught on the first stair-step. He turned to the old servant-woman. He wanted to ask her something, but his tongue refused to obey. To have something to say, he said, "Before I go up, I'd like to know the rent."

"It will be twenty riksdalars a year, but twelve for a half-year, sir. Please…"

"Cold, dismal, cutting words! But I am ashamed not to go up, now that I am here," he thought. He flew up the stairs.

His guide took him to the two little rooms with rose wall-paper. "Please sit down and inspect them," she said, and walked out, locking the door.

"Sit down? No, certainly not. Great God, what am I doing here? Which room? Nice? Heavenly nice! It's freshly scrubbed. Was it scrubbed last night? Orderly. Clean. With spring-fresh curtains put up. It appears that a guest was expected. And wallflowers in the window. Look, what mirrors in frames. Frames of glass, too, with gold underlayment. Just so. And the inner room? Rosy wall-paper there, too? But in a different way. Oh! One who gets to live here, and…if… which is to say, if… Good God! It was fairly certain that these were the rooms she dreamt of that night in Arboga, when…"

The door opened. She walked in. The sergeant moved a little aside at the appearance of a girl in black: a girl in ratine with Sara's face, gently smiling when she noticed his surprise. There was a finely starched collar on her breast. Her cheeks were pale. "I am in mourning, as you see," she said.

"How happy I am! You're alive? You're smiling?" he cried.

The grief, of which she spoke, sat like a fine haze above her eyes. But the whites shone blue-white, as they always had before, with the pupils glittering. "Albert," she said.

He did not answer, but merely gazed.

How do like these rooms? Do you want to rent them? But you can't know them much yet. Can't I invite you down to my place, now, so you can see how I live? Breakfast is waiting. And if you don't go on traveling today, I'd like to ask you to dinner. Would all that be acceptable, Albert?"

He still said nothing. But in all of his expression lay the answer: "It is acceptable."

**NOTES:**

The story "It Is Acceptable" was concluded, and Richard Furumo, who, through the last chapter had held his head half-lowered with a meditative, dreamy look, merely staring before him, now raised his head bolt upright, with his eyes mildly resting on the hunting lodge's director. He said nothing.

"Was there no more?" burst out Sir Hugo.

"No, not now."

"Then that is the remarkable little story, which I've never heard before, but about which I've heard both good and bad? It's indefensible that Richard did not let me know about it long ago, and run it in the Lodge's annals. As far as the content is concerned, they say that it has set all of Sweden into an uproar from its first appearance, but the thing has grown so widespread, that the younger generation, in general, take it for granted. I want to remind you, too, and the foreign press has noticed too; that this insignificant little piece has gone to the forefront of a trend in novels in Sweden, or seems to constitute the beginning of it, here in the fatherland. What do you say?"

Furumo still kept silent, as always, when ethical questions are revealed that he had seldom or never understood.

Frans Löwenstjärna, who otherwise wasn't slow to speak about ethical matters, held back; perhaps because he saw himself surrounded by the entire Cabinet of Ministers of the government, who were present during the narration.

Fortunately for Hugo, it happened that the minister in charge of Fine Art stepped up, turned to the chairman, and asked to say a few words.

The Sergeant-at-arms recognized him with a cheerful nod.

"I have asked to speak," he said, "only to add a footnote to the story of 'It is Acceptable'. When Furumo's story was printed the first time, it was so rudimentary, that it had not even been divided into chapters, and it had only 'One Week' for a title. When it was reprinted, it was divided into chapters, just as Sir

Richard presented it this afternoon. But the publisher had, moreover, appended an introduction…"

"An introduction?" cried Sir Hugo. "What did it say? I heard no such thing today."

"It doesn't belong to the piece, itself, and is not by Mr. Furumo, from what I know."

"How does the added introduction sound? Does the prime minister know about it? Or perhaps, you, Richard?"

"No," he answered, "Of course I have seen it in printed copies, but no more."

"Then I can tell you about it," resumed the minister. "During my studies in ethics I, too, could not avoid a connection to 'It Is Acceptable', and I am among those who happen to own a copy of it."

"Good, then can I get a bit of the introduction, as much as deserves to be heard?"

"Fortune has smiled upon us. When I knew that Sir Richard would present his manuscript this afternoon, I brought along… out of curiosity… my rare little book."

"My God, sir, let's hear what the attachment is all about!"

The young student took the book from his pocket, leafed through it, eyes gleaming, and finally opened to the title page, and said, "May I read aloud?"

"Yes, certainly, my friend!"

"The introduction, which, in the second edition, was added before the piece, itself, sounds like this:

They say that a thin veil hangs before Europe's future, preventing us from clearly seeing the figures behind it, waving to us. I believe that. The veil is not completely transparent; in some places the beautiful drapery hangs in somewhat thicker folds than others. So much less can be seen there. It would be lowly of us to be too curious about such a huge subject. And it would be arrogant if we should say we could express with certainty what lives behind the veil, in a yet unborn time, and express with certainty that which God has hidden. But, just the same, on that path that we ourselves and our children must walk, it is of human value, and necessary for us, to understand as much as is needed to proceed in the right direction. No one may, and no one can know Individual events to be met in the future. But the general trend... where the path is leading... is clearly indicated. That veil of secrecy is only half-way a jealous and impenetrable screen: It reveals the road, but not what is along the way. We may discern more and more of those things, as we hurry into the future."

"A person must, at some time, come to know himself. That cannot be helped. The more uprightly the better. I cannot believe differently. What, then, have been the use of millennia-old falsehoods? Society is trembling in its very foundations. What fruit have individuals harvested of this ceaseless hypocrisy to which they have been forced? Forced, I say. Yes, the fruit has become true immorality, with the title of morality. It came with another fruit: true unhappiness with the title of happiness."

"It's clear that what we are discussing must pertain to our time's problems that generally come to question, or some of them. It's these subjects that we can postpone, but not avoid. It's the sort of thing that all people think about, but no one dares speak of. It's the same sort which, if and when it is spoken, is much is poorly described, poorly disseminated, shackled, and condemned; for it contains one of the seeds of humanities rescue, in moral terms. And history can demonstrate very few examples where the peoples' teachers, taken en mass, did not always flee from what arrived to help, detested the means of rescue, and called the rescue itself destruction; and on the other hand, called everything that stood to offer assistance 'evil', sanctifying that in the name of goodness. When a time's work constantly goes to rescuing, helping, and improving the soul, they constantly shout that the times are determined by the world. They don't see that their own morality leads to real vices, or at least does not hinder them. We are not stating this as a fact; views can be whatever they are. We defame no one, we wish blessing on all."

"But as far as those subjects are concerned, that lie in the times to come; one may weep if he wants, but he cannot prevent them. Humanity's and morality's gradual salvation cannot be avoided."

"One can well say that humanity is collapsing under material interests, and becoming all the more worldly. One can only say, that so long as one fails to realize that it is our very souls that our times themselves strive for, most of all. It is the salvation of the beautiful, and innocent, that is the basis of our spirit. It is the experience of what is, in truth, good, and the idealistic hope that God allows us, because he created it. That is the question, for once. The defense of the only thing on earth that people value, or should value. A utopia, unrealized for millennia. So, does one call *that* interest, worldly? Does any meaning lie in the expression? On the other hand, we have an interest, in catching some glimpse of heaven on earth. A glimpse that God must want us to wish for, because he, himself created it. But people chased away that glimpse of heaven, and chase it away still, as much they are able, for they think it's necessary to make themselves unhappy, mostly. Not unhappy in small way; to the contrary, nearly all institutions set out to help in the small sense, to insure us ownership of the insignificant, to make us happier in smallness. They hardly achieve their goal to make us happy in larger sense, and they make real happiness a pure impossibility. The initial cause of that peculiar conflict is something certainly worthy of consideration; but its results threaten to dissolve humanity, and drive away all morality, and happiness as well. What can it be, that was intended to be respectable, that in its result became so dangerous? Through misunderstanding of what morality and happiness are, in themselves, according to true human nature, people believed themselves only capable of fostering fundamental religiosity in constant association with that which destroys the personality: That is to say, the person, in all forms, such as the individual, is crushed and annihilated. People believed that morality lies only in the general, which they therefore have called the pure. They did not see that of all of the personality's peculiarities, it is solely the reprehensible that is

108

against creation's true meaning in a person. But everything else individual about a person, far from needing to be dispelled, is itself the one condition for the person to be what he ought to be. So they stand there with all their respectable well-meaning, with the result that good morals don't germinate despite the crushing and humiliation of the individual. Nor is it through abysses of agony, that any right morality is attained. Then, is the winning of pure morality an unattainable treasure for the human being? By our expectations, the puzzle of morality must be solved at the same time as the puzzle of happiness. It is mankind's highest quest to find harmony between real, true morality, and real, true happiness, in the larger sense? If at some time, or for some special case, both cannot be united, but one of the two must be set aside until later, then let it be happiness that proceeds, for morality is more important then. For that thought, we die and become martyrs. But to strive to win harmony in both must be society's only great goal. All else is false or petty. To suffer needlessly for that right is a false martyrdom, it is deemed cowardly among people, and it is damnable by God. The Christian community may no longer paste-on the heathen ideas of revenge and public sacrifice, which no one, fundamentally, deserves, and of which, Christ made an end: if only we followed him!

What we have said so far, ought to be put into wider practice. But, we still can't look at dissertations on these subjects, or even wish to. People are fooling themselves if they believe that scientific systems, which serve some people well, can be written before-hand for everything. One must first come to know the human beings, themselves. See them at all their angles and corners. Listen to their most secret sighs, and not be disdainful at their tears of joy. In short, it is faithful narratives, pictures of life, that we need, such as collections, and observations. We can make whatever comment we like about those observations. We may condemn them, or we may regard them as dangerous. On the other hand, if the observations are real, then, regardless of whatever peculiarities they may have, they constitute precisely the necessary foreground, the indispensible condition for a true knowledge on the subject. For, then one begins to have something upon which to discourse. Then one can begin to say what should be rejected and what should be appreciated. On that foundation, endowed with inner experience of the person, philosophy may create the system, develop, teach, and advise completely, and in all of its dimensions. One could argue that philosophers, and legislators have followed that scheme for all times, but that is historically untrue. Only a few, at most, (mostly in ancient times) have acquired knowledge of the human being from life itself, as a source, and written about it. Since then, philosophers by the thousands have drawn conclusions, and built systems in cloistered studies, and through merely reading what others have discovered. They are fairly note-worthy for comprehending the philosopher's own biographies, and hermitic thought processes, but they are real flagellation and spiritual destruction for humanity when they succeed in making them operative in society. We shall deeply revere, and fall down in the dust for the philosophy when it once comes into being.

The manuscript that I present here contains the story of just one series of events. Naturally, not everything that happens in those events can pertain directly to the subject. Therefore, it cannot serve alone as a basis for any discourse, which should always fill that requirement for complete understanding of its predetermined goal. But it would please me if the events do not seem too paltry, to the reader, and the people who experienced them not too inhuman, or too insignificant. What they say to each other, and what they do, at least at first hand, means really nothing more than that. Yet, what they say to each other, and how they act in these events, is an experience; a fact; a slice of life. To condemn, or to approve that fact is the subject of this dissertation. However, what they say, and how they act has a bearing on something else, something other than the story. We meet, here, the modern 'noli me tangere' [touch me not]. The blossom of the century is a sensitive mimosa, whose touchy nerves shiver, and it hastily draws itself together around its

110

flower for every hand, however bold, cold and dirty, that attempts to touch such a chaste blade with its fingers. She loves to be understood, but not to be touched.

This follows the story, 'It is Acceptable', itself.

"Thank you", said Sir Hugo, after it had been read through. "But now I ask you, Minister, to openly say if 'It is Acceptable' is a "trend piece", as has been asserted from all sides."

""I must answer that question with a categorical 'no'"", answered the president. "Some see it as fairly praise-worthy, for a composition to be 'trendy'. Others hold it to be, from an artistic point of view, a fault. I say in both cases that 'It is Acceptable', like all of the other of Furumo's novels and short stories, is not a "trend piece"."

"Many of them are regarded as such, and 'It is Acceptable' in particular, from what I've heard", interjected Sir Hugo. "Where does that come from, then?"

"That has no basis other than a mistake, caused by, above all, the fact that people don't seem to have figured out what they mean by 'trend'."

"In the arts it is a pretty immediate question. Undoubtedly, everything in the world must have a trend, if the word, purely and simply means 'direction'; but not if speaking in an artistic sense."

"No, certainly not. When reflection, maxims, or doctrines occur in a piece, without being expressed by the piece's own characters; or if they are expressed by some among them, but the opinions are of a sort with content and tone that does not belong to the person's character who spoke them; or, even if they are part of a person's character, but are not completely motivated by the situation and circumstances in which they are spoken, (which is to say, that the individual has no cause or reason to speak them); the teachings in all of these cases, however good they may be, in and for themselves, have, however, been inartistically interjected into the piece, and create what one calls, stated poorly, 'trend-being'. They stand there, so to speak, only for the author's, or more rightly said, for the doctrine's sake as such,

111

which is out of place, because such teachings belong to science, but not art. Those just-named cased do not occur in 'It is Acceptable'; for those maxims are expressed by, among others, the piece's active character, Sara. They agree fully with her character and have their motives entirely in the situation or event. She has, you see, good reason to say them when she does. The doctrines, then, do not lie outside the piece, and are not just inserted. They do not constitute parasitic additions. On the contrary, they show themselves to be part of the piece's artistic whole, and are not there for the author's or the doctrine's account, but as ingredients in the depiction, namely, the prominent characters' self-confidence, or way of thinking. That is not to deny it, and say that no tenets, or thoughts in a piece, coincide with an author's own, or even that they hold good standing in the area of science. It would be all too strange, if the piece's characters did not come to some thought similar to the story-teller's himself, at some time or another; or if they all should be so foolish, that nothing of what they say could strike in with the demands of science's and with genuine truth. But the thing is this alone: that the credos and opinions that occur in an artistic piece, are not there for the dogma's, or their content's sake, but for character development and vivid reporting. On the other hand, in a dissertation, it is: In a scientific piece, everything that is reflective and doctrinal stands for its own account. Then, the important thing is thesis presentation, and system description.

"I understand well enough", said Sir Hugo, "That must constitute one of the principle differences between art and science, and that the former cannot have 'tendency-spirit' within it. All artistic pieces must have 'tendency' in a good or simple meaning, (merely as 'direction'). For example, The Iliad had the tendency to show the Greek's war with the Trojans, up to the fall of Hector. The Aeneid has a tendency to retell of how Aeneas came to Italy and settled his people in Latium. Gerusalemme Liberata has the tendency to sing the praises of the occupation of Jerusalem. The Henriad… but what am I saying? All such mean nothing to the person who is speaking in terms of trend in an artwork, for it pertains purely and simply to the conditions that the work has to address, which must be both innocent and indispensible."

"Therefore", continued the other, "the 'spirit of the trend', as far as it is something one speaks of in the sense of a quality, must, always include faults; be a parasitic outgrowth. When you hear people praise novels, dramas, or other lyrical pieces for such, it comes only as a misunderstanding, or unclear perception of the subject."

"But Mr. Minister!" interjected the chamberlain, leaning his handsome head a little. "It cannot be denied that poetic, or, as we say here, artistic pieces can be quite instructive. Does one not feel inner joy in the soul when that happens?"

"Without a doubt."

"Can't one enjoy good maxims, regardless of from whose mouth, and in what form they are spoken?"

"Of course."

"Don't stories and poetry exercise great power in general? Novels, where they follow the current of the times, in the spirit of the new times, and in the service of progress, extensively prepare the sensibilities and thought patterns of the coming generation. Before you know it, through something that could be called "opinion's stream composition", it finds itself in a completely different place within civilization than you expected, and your father described. It is even often the case that the reading of novels, and in particular the more meaningful ones, brings on admirable transformations in the old, themselves. Many of them feel much of their prejudices and older presuppositions tumble end-over-end. They are enchanted, and become young a second time, as has happened to me, myself."

"Undeniably."

"What difference are we talking about, then," Mr. Minister? Good learning is always good learning?"

"That is so," he answered. "Theses and maxims can always be instructive, whether they are in artistic pieces, or scientific pieces. The difference lies merely in that those in the former case constitute a part of character and event description, but in the latter a description of a thought system."

"Hmm. I understand."

"Therein lie the differences, but they are alike, in that in both cases they can be powerful and instructive."

"Well, still a 'trend novel'?"

"That could seem so, too, of course, but just as it is worse for its own genre, because it is neither pure art, nor pure science, its power is greatly weakened. Certainly, a 'trend novel', written with talent, can make a temporary impression. It lives largely in the moment. A truly artistic piece, on the other hand, has qualities that never die."

"In truth, sir…"

But the lively student did not let himself be hindered from developing his point, which he had only begun, and even repeated himself a little. "Ordinarily," he said, "people believe that they have only 'trend novels' to thank for that sort of influence on society's opinions, and the transformations that we are discussing; since what one calls 'trend' lies in a bunch of interlarded doctrines, lore, and maxims, which the reader then uses for information and guidance. Therein, however, lies a big mistake. Novels mean far more when they are truly artistic, which is to say, when they are free of all outgrowths and parasitic off-shoots of opinions; namely those that don't belong to the work itself, but are injected as the author's special thinking of his own. That includes when the people and actions, themselves, occur merely as mouth-pieces for the author; a sort of manikin set up in diverse positions, to thereby impart certain truths upon the reader. In the Arts, such things are foreign and fallacious, even if one cheaply pleads to be well-meaning and instructive, as is discussed here. The mischief of 'trend spirit' lies in a will to preach with the artist's mouth. Can't one obtain knowledge from a work, then, just because it is an artwork? Question: Why can't such books be instructive, too? The answer is that one can learn from them… and learn a lot! But, not in a way borrowed from science. Teachings become confused and often false, when doctrines that they convey are inappropriately blended into an artistic project, instead of brought forth in true logical form, which happens when science, itself, prefers the dogmas, in and from a system. But, one may also ask how art can be purely and simply instructive? The answer: the same way as events and personal characters in the real world can be quite informative to observe, hear, and take in, without any attached scraps of paper with conclusions, judgments, morals, maxims and opinions. And, to go a step further; may not all of these flesh and blood people, and all of these observed events make so much deeper impression, just because such parasitic notes are not pasted all over them? Can't they be rich and instructive? Without a doubt! So, not so differently; even an art-work can, and should be instructive, when it is genuine and real. As soon as it becomes a question of a reflection's truth, in and for itself, then it stands in the area of science. The reason it is so important not to mix science's with art's presentations, lies in just that. For a dogma's truth to be found, it must be seen, and tested in its relation to the system in general, which cannot happen except within science itself. In that great and important difference, for both art and science, authors in general seem to not give much attention. They even seem as if they, in the creation of their poems, dramas, novels, not even once understood, or knew of it. Because of that, their characters often lack flesh and blood, (they are not individuals, but just stereotypes; *loci communes*-people), and their actions have no real life. Because both characters, and actions merely appear as cloud-pictures; as pale shadows of opinions, they actually belong in a completely different land, the land of science. The 'post-art', as they call trend-poetry (whether it is novels, dramas, or lyrics) have, as a short-coming, paid too little attention to this difference that we are discussing. The author, male or female, finds it necessary to be instructive. Wonderful! Then why don't they write a dissertation on the subject? Then the matter would be in the right place. 'Yes,' they answer, because dissertations

115

are read by no one, but novels by many. So, when we want to serve the public with education, we choose the media that hits home with people. That has a new flaw. People would much rather read good treatises than bad novels, and the best part is that they get far better spiritual benefit from them."

"Good," said Sir Hugo as he looked around with a jovial expression, and stood up. He took the Prime Minister's hand, and shook it warmly and declared the meeting adjourned.

After he kissed his sisters and their children, he wanted to get away from the hall, and work in the garden before he went off to bed. But then, at the door, his eye fell upon Richard Furumo.

"Listen!" he cried, "I would have a word with you before we part this evening. I want to thank you for what you said today. But now I must request that the next time we meet for literary talks, let's have some of another pre-determined piece, of which I, myself, only know fragments through one and another name in our Songes, and which I desire to both hear, and to give complete coverage in my next edition of the 'Hunting Lodge'. After that's done, you are to come here with only new things: Purple counts, silk rabbits and such, for which, I... I admit it... feel the greatest longing."

"What sort of piece would milord request?"

"I'm not really sure of the name," answered Sir Hugo, "But from what I've heard I believe the 'Sensible Critic' called it 'Tales of Death'."

"Aha!" said Richard. "It is about Murni-books?"

"Fairly possible they could be called that."

"The subject," continued the other, "partly concerns antique galleries, but for the most part, the events occur in the spirit world."

"In the spirit world? Exactly. I had sensed already in the Songes, that it should be so. What do you think, Eleonora? Frans, Aurora... into the spirit world, Kids!"

"Farewell, farewell until we meet again!"

THE END